THE RESORT

M J HARDY

MORE BOOKS BY M J HARDY

The Girl on Gander Green Lane

The Husband Thief

Living the Dream

The Woman who Destroyed Christmas

The Grey Woman

Behind the Pretty Pink Door

The Resort

You're Invited!

Join my Newsletter

Follow me on Facebook

THE RESORT

M J Hardy

When three women win a holiday in a Facebook
competition, they think it's by chance.
It's not.
When one woman accompanies her husband on business,
she thinks she'll return with him.
She won't.
Welcome to the resort where nothing is as it seems.
On the outside, it's heaven on earth. A dreamy romantic
getaway, with pristine sandy beaches, glorious sunshine, and
glamorous accommodation.
The perfect lover's hideaway with uninterrupted views over
a freshwater lagoon.
Nothing to do but enjoy the ultimate pamper experience on
a ridiculously dreamy holiday of a lifetime.
That's what they think.
Who will survive the week and who won't leave at all?

QUOTE

You will never understand the damage you did to someone
until the same thing is done to you. That's why I'm here.
Karma

CHAPTER 1

KIM

I've always loved the airport. I associate it with happy memories, holidays, relaxation, sun and exotic places. Most of all, I associate it with spending time with Jack. Lots of lovely time with my husband, who never seems to have that much of it at home.

"Kim, hurry up, a couple just pushed in and I'm about to blow a fuse."

Dragging my wheelie case behind me, I up my pace because as usual Jack's on a mission. He is always uptight at this stage of the journey, so I don't give it much thought. Once we're on the plane, he will relax, but I know he won't until then.

As we wait, I check out the other passengers and my heart lurches when I see a family a few steps ahead of us. A beautiful baby who can't be more than a few weeks old is being rocked by her doting father, who looks so proud it brings a smile to my face. The fact the baby is dressed head to toe in pink gives her sex away and I look with envy as the mother holds the hand of another pretty girl, who must be around 4 years old.

Perfect.

I stare at them, unable to drag my eyes away from a scene that I wish was mine so hard it hurts. I want a family like that. A contented husband, proud of his girls. The way he gazes at his baby with pride and the way his wife looks at him and smiles, her gaze full of love and happiness.

"Bloody hell, I hope they're not anywhere near us. The last thing we need is a crying baby all the way, that would be just my luck."

Jack sounds annoyed and his frown and shiver of displeasure reminds me we are poles apart in what we want from life. I don't even answer him and just stare hungrily at a scene I want more than anything and as the line shifts, I feel the sharp pain of a suitcase being shoved in my back.

"I'm sorry." I turn quickly and see a woman looking apologetic.

I just smile and turn away as Jack hisses, "We'll be lucky to get there at all at this rate. Did you remember to book the lounge, I need a stiff gin and tonic after this debacle?"

"Yes."

He nods and turns his attention back to the slowest line in history and I glance across at the first-class check-in desk and wish we were in a position to travel that way.

The woman that stands studying her perfectly manicured nails, looks as if she just left the spa. Long blonde hair curled in those large waves that appear to be all the rage, make her look as if she just stepped out of the hairdresser's chair. She is wearing a beautiful pale blue trouser suit with a white silk camisole under the jacket, clutching a Chanel handbag as her husband loads the belt with their Louis Vuitton luggage. I feel a pang of envy as I look at a woman I wish I could be and just pray that her husband is old and ugly.

As he turns and smiles at the glamorous woman, my heart skips a beat. He is utterly gorgeous. Dressed in a smart jacket and chinos, he looks as if he's just stepped out of Heat magazine. His hair is dark and well styled and he looks to be around his mid-forties. I watch with interest as he slips an arm around the woman's waist possessively, and as he whispers in her ear, she nods and looks around with an air of boredom.

"Hurry up Kim, for god's sake what's the matter with you today?"

Jack's voice tears my attention away from the couple and I follow him to the nearest available check-in desk.

As always, he removes the plastic wallet from his man bag and hands over the necessary paperwork, preparing to charm the woman who smiles at him coyly. Yes, Jack is a good-looking man himself, and when he wants to be, he can charm the honey from a bee.

"Any chance of an upgrade?"

He stares at the woman with a mischievous wink and she blushes prettily. "I'll just check, sir."

She looks down and Jack leans on the counter, dipping his head a little closer and I can almost hear her deep breathing from where I'm standing. I know why he's doing it; he's always using his charm to grab a freebie. The best table in the restaurant, an extra serving of food, the best seat in the theatre, always the best of everything he can blag for free.

"We only have one seat in premium economy. I'm sorry, sir, the flight is almost full."

He nods. "I'll take it."

She looks past him to me and I see a flash of irritation in her eyes as I just smile with embarrassment.

"May I ask if you, or your wife will be taking the premium seat?"

"Me, of course, I work on the flight. Kim just watches the entertainment and reads trashy magazines."

"Thank you, sir."

Jack turns to me and looks pleased. "You don't mind, do you darling? I've got a ton of work I need to get through and if I get it done on the plane, it will free up my time at the resort."

"It's fine."

I turn away and wonder for the umpteenth time about my husband. I know he's selfish, inconsiderate and impatient, but somehow I still manage to love him despite his flaws. Just a smile and the odd hint of affection makes me forgive him, and I still count myself lucky that we met and married within six months of meeting. That was ten years ago and largely I've been happy except for his slightly wandering eye and the fact we still don't have children.

As we head towards the security line, I feel a sinking feeling inside. Maybe I should use this time wisely. Wait for him to be in a good mood and broach the subject of adoption. It's obvious there's something wrong somewhere down the line because according to all the tests I've had, the problem doesn't lie with me. The trouble is, Jack refuses to get tested, telling me he doesn't have a problem and it must lie with me.

My heart sinks when we reach another line and Jack growls angrily. "Great, another long wait. I blame you for this, Kim, if you had booked us fast track check-in, we would be nursing a gin by now, not waiting in line with the rest of the peasants. Honestly, you should shape up and pre-plan a lot more, just saying."

He stares moodily at his Apple watch, and I hate the fact I bite my tongue to avoid a scene. Then again, I'm used to that and wonder when I became so weak. I never used to be this person. I was always prepared to stand up and speak my mind when required, but over the years Jack has eroded any self-confidence I had and it's just easier to stay silent. Maybe it's because the older I get, the more I fear him leaving me. I don't earn much as a hairdresser and Jack has always brought in the lion's share and thinking of struggling on my own is not a pleasant thought, so I just push aside any doubts and carry on as if I'm happy.

But I'm not.

In fact, I am so unhappy I feel as if something has got to give and I'm fearful of that because I don't like change and never have, so maybe this holiday is just what we need to work out the finer details because it's make or break time for Jack and Kim and if I'm sure of anything, it's that Jack hasn't got a clue about that.

CHAPTER 2

*H*iding a smile, I follow a furious Jack to the airport lounge in dire need of a gin and tonic. I found it mildly amusing when he was stopped and searched and half of his possessions were confiscated. He couldn't even blame me because he was insistent on packing his own bag and obviously didn't think the half litre bottle of gin, expensive aftershave and Swiss army knife would be a problem. The fact he argued with the security guard almost got him arrested and as he strides in front of me, I struggle not to laugh.

As we power through the crowds in duty free, I notice the elegant woman perusing the expensive perfumes. I expect they got fast-tracked through security because she has quite a selection of designer pleasures in her basket to brighten her day. Her partner is patiently holding it as she contemplates another purchase and he waits patiently as if he is happy to run around after her while she spends a small fortune.

The only thing that interrupts Jack in his pursuit of alcohol, is a display of expensive watches and as he falters, my heart sinks because Jack thinks nothing of charging an expensive watch to his credit card to 'cheer himself up' and then we spend the rest of the year paying for it.

I know better than to argue and as he decides on yet another one, I wander off to study the make-up and decide on a nail varnish that catches my eye.

Finally, we make it to the lounge and as Jack takes a deep slug of his drink, he finally raises a smile.

"Well, I needed that."

"Yes, it's always stressful travelling. Never mind, at least you have a decent seat and can relax now."

He nods and looks apologetic. "I'm sorry about the upgrade, you don't mind, do you? It's just that I have a ton of work to get through and I can't concentrate with screaming children distracting me."

"It's fine, I'll probably sleep, anyway."

He smiles and looks relieved. "So, tell me about this resort, I still can't believe this is happening at all. Are you sure it's all free? I would hate to get there and discover you made your usual mistake of not reading the small print."

Pushing away the sharp reply I really want to answer him with, I smile. "Yes, it's all free and I still can't believe we won. I've entered shed loads of those Facebook competitions and never actually won before. I always thought they were scams but apparently not."

"Well, I'm not complaining. One week all-inclusive at the Lotus Lake Resort and Spa is just what the doctor ordered. What do you know of the place?"

"Not a lot, really. I googled it and apparently its new. It hasn't officially opened to the public yet and we are the guinea pigs, as they say. It's why they ran the competition. To test out the facilities, all expenses paid in return for our feedback at the end. You know, I've heard some people make a living out of this."

"Then where do I apply?" Jack smiles and any irritation I

have towards him dissolves in an instant. When he wants to be, Jack can be so charming I forget my own name. It's probably why I stay because Jack Parker is special in a lot of ways and I am madly in love with him. When he's tired and irritable, I could hammer him to death like a psychopath but like now, when he is calm, charming and sexy, I would do anything he asked because I am so in love with my husband, it blinds me to all his flaws and despicable character traits. He is forgiven in an instant and I would never dream of swapping him for anyone else, because who could hold a candle to this man, anyway?

By the time we reach our seats on board, I am in my happy place. Jack disappears to premium economy, and I am left to find my seat towards the rear of the aircraft, just praying I get a window seat and a space beside me. It's not looking good when I see how full the plane is and when I finally locate my seat, I notice with a sinking feeling that I'm beside the aisle next to a couple who appear to be arguing. He is also impossibly large and just thinking of the journey spent squashed in beside him is not a pleasant one but as usual, I suck it up and smile apologetically as my eyes fall to his bag occupying my seat.

"I'm so sorry, I think this is my seat."

The flash of irritation on the woman's face doesn't make for a good start as she nudges the man and hisses, "Move your fucking bag."

He grunts and thrusts it on her lap and she screeches. "Not on me you idiot, put it up top."

"No room." He grunts and as I look, my heart sinks when I see he's right. The overhead lockers are already stuffed full, and I'm not happy about the prospect of having my own small cabin bag between my legs for the journey.

Catching the eye of the stewardess, I say apologetically, "Excuse me, but is there somewhere I can stow this bag?"

She heads across and smiles. "Oh dear, it's not looking good. Let me see what I can do."

She heads off and I struggle into my seat to wait because the plane is still filling up and I know the next eight hours are going to be excruciating.

I feel a sharp shove behind me as my seat is pushed forward and I grit my teeth as the person grabs the back of it, along with my hair, as they edge into their row. The person in front tests out the seat's recline function and I envision a journey squashed beside a man who smells distinctly off and a person in front who is obviously intent on sleeping on my lap for most of it. Counting to ten slowly in my mind, I wait for the stewardess to take my bag at least and it feels like an age before she returns and smiles.

"If you come with me, madam, I've found you a seat with more space."

"Thank God for that." The man beside me mumbles and I couldn't agree with him more.

I follow her back down the aisle and noting the crowded plane, feel surprised that she's managed to pull this one off at all. As we reach the galley, we step aside to let the family of four pass and I smile at the woman who is laughing at something her daughter is saying. She returns it and once again I think how lucky she is as they slide into a row with the bulkhead in front of them and make it look so easy I feel ashamed of myself. The stewardess leans in and whispers, "It's your lucky day, I had a note from check-in to see if we could swap your seat. The agent on the desk was most insistent."

"She was?" I stare at her in surprise and she throws me a sympathetic look. "Yes, she told my FSM that you had been split up from your husband and felt bad for you. Well, luckily, we have a better seat and your journey will be a much better one. Follow me."

We head through the cabin and reach the premium

section and it already feels more spacious despite being a much smaller cabin. It's like venturing into a different world after the chaos of the economy section. Quickly, I look for Jack and see him chatting to the woman beside him, who is throwing him a look I have seen a thousand times before, and my heart sinks. Great, now I've got that image in my head for the entire journey of Jack flirting with a woman who looks happy to join the mile high club. I pointedly look away and hope I'm not anywhere near them because he is really starting to aggravate me and I want to enjoy this experience of a lifetime.

To my surprise, we carry on and I stare around in shock as she directs me to a seat in first class and smiles. "Here you are, 5B. It's not a window seat I'm afraid, but it's way better than the one you were in."

"Are you sure I can sit here?" I stare at her in disbelief and she laughs. "Of course, it's going spare and quite honestly, if anyone needed it, it was you. Just enjoy it, I know I would."

She nods towards my case. "Would you like me to help you with that?"

"It's fine – thank you. In fact, I can't thank you enough, this is, well, it's amazing."

She winks and says brightly, "Enjoy. Anyway, I should go, I think we're about to close up."

I stare around me in surprise as a warm feeling spreads through me. First class all the way this time. If only Jack could see me now.

As I make myself comfortable, it's not long before another stewardess heads my way and hands me a glass of champagne. "Enjoy your flight, madam, if you need anything, don't hesitate to ask."

She smiles warmly and moves on, leaving me in an extremely happy place as I settle back and sigh with relief.

Sometimes Karma plays a blinder, and this is one huge middle finger to Jack who would be green with envy if he could see me now.

CHAPTER 3

*A*fter possibly the best flight of my life, I feel fully rested as I make my way off the plane. It feels so different exiting a flight that has proven to be an experience I am unlikely to recover from anytime soon. The space I had to stretch out and relax in my own private cabin was unexpected. Then there were the delicious meals and fine wines. A larger entertainment screen and gorgeous amenity kit with top end toiletries and superior items were a delightful treat compared to the usual plastic rubbish. The cabin was calm and not crowded at all, and even the toilets were clean and crammed full of expensive soap and luxurious hand lotion. In fact, I feel as if the holiday started at Heathrow and I wonder what it's like to travel this way every time.

Luckily, Jack has disembarked already and after thanking the crew profusely, I make my way to the Arrivals hall. Jack is already in line and I watch him chatting to the woman who sat beside him on the plane and feel a sharp pang as I realise that to any other onlooker, they are a couple.

The elegant man and woman are behind me, and I try to listen in on their conversation while we wait. They were in first class too but nowhere near me and yet when I stretched my legs, I stole many looks at them and vowed to try to be just a fraction of the woman I appear to have developed a fixation for. She even travelled elegantly and changed into lounge wear and wore a cashmere looking eye mask while she slept most of the way. Subsequently, she now looks as if she's stepped out of a magazine as her trouser suit is not creased in the slightest and her hair gleams as it swings around her shoulders. The man appeared to work beside her for most of the flight and looks happy as he entwines his fingers in hers as they wait, with none of the impatience that Jack displays.

"Is it far?" The woman's soft voice wafts towards me and he says with a clipped accent, "Half an hour away, I think. They said a car would be waiting."

"Good, hopefully they can fit us in for a massage today, I think my back is in knots after that flight."

"I could email them if you like."

"Super, darling."

He taps a message on his phone and I sigh inside. This man is my dream man and if I could be that woman, I would die happy.

It doesn't take me long to get through passport control and I head across to Jack who is waiting to reclaim our suitcases.

"Hey, darling, did you have a good flight?"

The woman beside him looks up sharply and I smile and slip my hand in my husband's, noting the frown on her face as I kiss him lightly on the cheek. "The best, how about you?"

"It was ok, they didn't have my meal choice, but it was edible at least."

Thinking of my own gourmet meal, I sigh with satisfaction. "Mine was lovely."

He turns his attention to the belt and sighs. "I bet ours are last off and to be honest, I can't wait a moment longer to relax by a pool and switch off."

"Me neither." He stares at me a little harder and shakes his head. "You know, Kim, there's something different about you since that flight, you seem so, well, chilled."

Thinking of the last eight hours of luxury, I smile. "I had a good sleep, maybe that's all I needed."

Running his hand around my waist, he pulls me close and whispers, "I can't wait to get there, you know how horny holidays make me."

"I know."

For a moment I could convince myself that everything was right with our marriage because when Jack's in this mood, nothing else matters. We are those newlyweds who doted on each other and the couple that fell in love madly and deeply. Yes, this holiday is just what was required and as he kisses me tenderly, surrounded by strangers in a sterile airport, I couldn't be happier.

~

WE FINALLY RETRIEVE our bags and as we head through customs, Jack says with concern, "Are you sure there's transport provided?"

"Yes, there should be someone to meet us."

I look anxiously at the many boards being held up and then spy one that says, **Lotus Lake Resort and Spa**.

"Over there."

Jack sighs with relief.

"Thank God for that, come on, final stage and then hello paradise."

We make our way over to the sign and the man holding it beams his welcome. "Welcome to Kurraga. If you head outside, you will see a minibus waiting with the resort name on the side. Someone will take your bags while you make yourself comfortable."

Feeling happy, relaxed and excited, we head outside and as the heat hits me, all my troubles dissolve in an instant.

Jack groans. "I needed that. Wow, how hot is this?"

"It's perfect."

The brand new gleaming mini bus waits patiently and as Jack entrusts our bags to the driver, we step on board and the first people I see are the glamorous couple from the plane. They look up and smile, and I don't miss the interest on Jack's face as he smiles at the woman first.

We take the seats behind them and Jack grins. "This is nice."

"It certainly is." He twists my fingers in his and raises my hand to his lips. "I can't wait for this."

As I settle beside my husband, all is good with the world, and I look with interest at the people who join us on board.

They all appear pleasant enough and as the door closes, the driver says jovially, "Welcome to the Lotus Lake Resort and Spa. I'm Eddie and I'll be driving you there today. It will only take 30 minutes and then your holiday can begin. Welcome to paradise."

As he fires up the engine, I settle back in my seat. I can't wait.

CHAPTER 4

EVELYN

*S*ighing, I shift in my seat and stare moodily out of the window. This is just great. A whole week with Charles, it's enough to drive me slowly mad. How I wish he was more interesting. Like the man who is sitting behind me who caught my eye in the airport. Now there's a man I would enjoy spending a week with. Good looking in a rough and ready way and I bet he's an animal in bed. The woman with him doesn't know how lucky she is. Yes, a real man, not the pander pony beside me who wouldn't even breathe if I tell him I've got a headache.

My life is so boring and I don't know what to do about it. When I married Charles, I thought I had it all. Wealth, a handsome husband and a life stretching in front of me of privilege and adventure. Funny how the dream gets distorted by reality. My life is one endless round of coffee mornings, shopping and visits to the spa which must be most women's idea of heaven. Not mine. I always wanted more than that, a career, something worthwhile to occupy my time and not to become a trophy wife, but that's how it turned out. Charles swept me off my feet and I was blinded by his wealth. He's good looking, charming, and a dream come true. Now the rosy glow has faded from my eyes, I realise how shallow it all is. There is so much more I want to do, but he won't hear a word of it.

"Darling…" He wraps his fingers around mine and whispers, "I have booked you in for that massage at 3pm, is that ok?"

"Yes, lovely darling."

I smile and he nods as if he's just wrapped up another business deal. Mindful of where we are, I say in a low voice, "Charles, I've been thinking."

He actually places his finger on my lips and whispers, "Tell me later, I have an email I need to answer as a priority. Maybe we can discuss your thoughts over a pre-dinner drink this evening."

I nod miserably and he starts tapping into his phone as I hear a giggle behind me and the low tones of a couple richer than I am in so many ways. "Stop that, what will everyone think?"

The tears well up as I imagine being as happy as the woman behind me clearly is. It's obvious they are. Who wouldn't be with a man like that beside them? If only mine gave me half as much attention as he gives his phone, I may not be so miserable.

Looking out of the window instead, I note with interest the landscape as we pass. As paradise goes, we've hit the jackpot here and I wonder about the man who made this trip possible. Lotus enterprises is the holding company of the resort we are going to. The fact we are here is by invite only because Charles has been managing this guy's investments for years. Now the resort is finally about to open and we have been invited to test out the facilities. Charles doesn't talk to me about business, so I don't know more than that, but I am interested to meet the man behind the dream.

Sighing, I lean back and look around me and a woman sitting across the aisle catches my eye and smiles. I smile back and wonder why she's here alone. I saw her in the baggage reclaim area as she hauled her suitcase from the belt and as shallow as it sounds, I liked the outfit she is wearing. Tight black skinny jeans, ripped at the knees, with a silk camisole and short fitted jacket. She has long dark wavy hair and the huge designer sunglasses perched on her head are an expensive brand. Her luggage was all coordinated and I sigh when I realise how much that impresses me. I really need to get a life because I am burning in material hell.

"Ladies and gentlemen, we have reached our destination." The driver calls out and I look with interest at the palatial resort looming up before us.

We sweep through huge white pillared gates and my first sight of paradise takes my breath away.

Charles looks up and nods with appreciation. "Looking good, then again, I never expected any less of him. That man has it all worked out and probably left nothing to chance."

"What's he like?"

"Ok, I guess, to be honest it's all business with him and he gives nothing away. Good business sense though, he keeps me on my toes, which is saying something."

He reaches out and twists his fingers in mine and says smoothly, "We'll check in and while you relax, I'll tick a few items off my to do list. This week should be fun."

He looks away and I die a little inside. Fun. I'm not sure if Charles knows the meaning of the word and all I can see is a week of boredom, while I try to remember why I married him in the first place.

As we disembark the mini bus, I look with interest at my fellow passengers, trying hard not to openly stare at the man who sat behind me.

He is so good looking and I feel a shiver of desire pass through me. Dark hair, piercing blue eyes and a body that I can tell would look good lying beside the pool. His wife, or at least I think they're married, is pretty with her blonde bob and simple shift dress. An understated elegance that makes me feel as if I'm way overdressed. She stands back a little as he looks around him with interest and for a moment, I catch his eye and feel a warm feeling spread through me as he smiles and something shifts between us.

"Come on darling, the porter will deliver our bags to the room."

Charles snakes his arm around my waist and guides me up the impressive white marble steps towards the reception that opens up into a vast space.

It feels so tranquil here, so beautiful and serene, I can feel the tension leave me almost immediately. I tune out as Charles jostles for position in the line and secures our room and a soft voice beside me says, "Wow, this place is impressive."

I turn to see the single woman beside me and she grins, holding out her hand. "Hi, I'm Emma."

"Evelyn."

I smile and she shakes my hand with a cool grip.

"I must say, I was blown away to win this competition."

"Competition?" I'm a little confused, and she laughs.

"Yes, can you believe I won this week away on a Facebook ad? All I had to do was comment and before I knew it, I had a message in messenger telling me I'd won. Crazy, isn't it?"

"That's amazing. You must be so happy."

"I am actually."

"Are you on your own?"

"Sadly, yes, although that's not unusual. I'm always on my own because I haven't met anyone I want to bother seeing twice. It must be nice to have found your other half." She sounds wistful, and as her eyes flick over to Charles, I see a little envy in her stare.

"Yes, it is."

My words betray me because I would give anything to be in her shoes, actually scrub that, I want to be in the petite blonde's shoes because my attraction to her husband has shocked me. I don't look at other men, I rarely even bother to acknowledge they are there. After all, I have a husband, despite how little I see of him.

Emma leans in and whispers, "Maybe there will be a single man here this week, perhaps this is destiny and I will find true love in paradise."

She winks and as Charles heads our way, says quickly, "It looks as if you've checked in. I had better fight my way to the front because I am itching to make it to that sunbed at some point today. Enjoy your stay."

She smiles. "I hope to catch up with you later, although don't worry, I'm not a weird hanger on, just come and find me if you want some girly company. Well, anyway, I should go and leave you to your holiday. Have a good one."

She heads off before Charles reaches us and he says quickly, "Who was that?"

"Her name's Emma, she won this holiday on Facebook."

"Oh yes, I heard he was running a competition for guinea pigs."

"Guinea pigs?"

"Yes, Mr Wheeler wanted to test out the facilities and grab some five-star reviews. He ran the competition on Facebook as a way of stirring up interest. Competition aside, the bookings are phenomenal and as I said before, that man knows what he's doing."

"Will he be here?"

Charles shrugs. "It's doubtful, he rarely stays in one place long enough to breathe. It certainly teaches me a thing or two about time management."

We step inside a lift that is pretty large and opulent. Mirrors line the wall and unconsciously I study my reflection with a critical eye. Perfect. Then again, that vision gives me more displeasure than if I had greasy hair and no make-up on wearing a dress that is stained and torn. I'm not sure when I hated the perfection my life brings. It crept up on me without me seeing it and now it's here, I look on my life with hatred and derision.

Charles punches the button for the floor we need, and I'm not surprised to see it's on the top one. He turns and winks.

"Only the best for us, darling, it pays to have contacts and Mr Wheeler has ensured we are in the best room."

"That's kind of him."

"I suppose, although I would have expected nothing less."

Charles smiles with the smug look of someone who expects perfection, which makes my heart sink. He looks at me that way too, I'm not stupid. I know he expects the same of me. The designer clothes, the modern tasteful home. The small fortune he expects to pay at the end of the month when he receives my credit card statement, showing him I have maintained the image of perfection by weekly visits to the hairdressers, beauticians and designer shops.

Charles expects perfection in every aspect of his life, even the bedroom. Sex with Charles is perfunctory, probably because he doesn't want to mess up my hair. It's cold, clinical and a tick on his to do list and afterwards he leaves me to shower while he answers any emails that came in during the ten minutes or so the phone wasn't in his hand.

The elevator arrives and as we step outside, I note the plush carpeting that still smells new and the freshly painted walls with not a mark on them. Charles stops at a large wooden door

21

that clearly states it's the penthouse, and I resist the urge to roll my eyes. I know I'm ungrateful and I hate myself for that too because I have it all and my only worry is getting through the day without losing my mind through boredom.

I follow him into a large airy space and catch my breath. This is outstanding.

Charles laughs softly beside me. "Yes, this will do. A panoramic sea view and a set of rooms suited to our needs."

He drops his bag on the table nearby and heads toward the double doors leading onto the balcony. As he opens them, I hear the crash of waves outside and as I follow him, I stare in amazement at a beach paradise. The balcony alone is worth a mention because it has its own hot tub and impressive sun loungers. It's absolutely huge and appears to be in its own little world as it juts out above the rest of the hotel.

The heat is almost unbearable and Charles leans across and presses a switch on the wall, initiating the fan on the ceiling.

"That's better."

He looks at me sharply. "Why don't you settle in and change into something more suitable. I'll grab us a couple of drinks and we can sit out here for a bit. I'm expecting a call from Paris that I need to take and then it will be time for your massage."

I nod and turn to leave and he says quickly, "Happy, darling?"

Sighing inside, I turn and smile weakly. "Of course, darling, thank you."

He nods and lifts his phone and as I walk away, I wonder how much longer I can do this.

CHAPTER 5

EMMA

This place is amazing. I actually can't believe I'm here at all and all because I commented on a Facebook ad.

I'm the last to check in and the receptionist smiles her welcome. "Miss Stone, it's a pleasure to meet you."

"Call me Emma." I smile warmly.

"This is absolutely gorgeous; I can't believe I'm here."

The woman nods. "It certainly is, I'm privileged to be part of the launch."

She consults her screen and as she taps away, I look around me in awe. Things like this don't happen to me. Emma Stone, the girl who never seems to catch a break. When I left school, I had zero qualifications because my parents dragged me halfway across the world just before my exams. My father got a job in Nigeria and it was decided that we would all go and enjoy the experience that living in another country brings. By the time we returned home, I had to enrol in college just to take my exams, which didn't go well. Subsequently, I left with no qualifications and resorted to working in a factory until I made the break and set up my own baking business.

Emma's cakes was born out of my rented kitchen and now I supply several farm shops and cater for corporate functions. Things could be better and money is tight, so I was ecstatic when I won this. Finally, I can relax for a week and recharge my exhausted batteries.

"Here you are, the president's suite. I hope you enjoy your stay."

She hands me the keys that hang from a white fluffy keyring and my business brain looks with disapproval at an item that will need replacing by the end of the week. Whoever thought white would be a good idea needs their head examining because after the sun cream, sticky fingers and general day-to-day dirt, this will soon look way past its best?

However, as my fingers curl around the soft fabric, I sigh with contentment. Perfect.

Thanking the receptionist, I head to the elevator after being assured my suitcase is in my room already and I feel an inner glow settling around me. This is relaxation at its finest and if only I could enjoy holidays like this always.

The fact I'm on my own is no hardship. I have my kindle and that's all I need, really. Maybe the odd conversation would be nice and Evelyn looks the sort who would appreciate that. I'm not sure why, but there's something sad about her. She disguises it well under a blank icy gaze, but I see it in her eyes. I'm not sure what she has to be sad about because her husband looks like a movie star and couldn't be more attentive if he tried. If only I met a man like that, I would be rich in so many ways.

I locate my room and as I step inside, I gasp with delight. President's suite is right because this room could house a small family. A huge four poster bed stands to one side in a room that is larger than my apartment at home. The view from the bifold doors takes my breath away and as I step out onto a large balcony, I could be in heaven. The view is outstanding and I spy the comfortable sun lounger with glee. Wow, this is paradise at its finest and I can't wait to explore.

Inside the room, sitting on a silver tray, is a frosted glass holding a brightly coloured cocktail with a small envelope nestling beside it. Intrigued, I lift it and tear it open, revealing a hand written card.

Welcome to Lotus Lake Resort and Spa.
We hope you enjoy your all-inclusive complimentary stay with us.
Call 505 for anything you need, night or day, and make sure you take advantage of all our facilities to make your stay memorable.

Well, that's one five-star review guaranteed already. I couldn't fault a thing if I tried.

Squealing with pleasure, I jump onto the bed and wave my legs and arms in the air in delight, as I sink into a glorious mattress that moulds around my body like a lover's embrace. I could get used to this and I'm already dreading going home - but I'm here now.

After a while, I quickly jump up and claim the record for changing into a bikini. I don't even unpack, I haven't time for that and grabbing my sarong and sunscreen, I head down to find the pool. I absolutely cannot waste a minute of this break and have to pinch myself that this is real at all.

As I walk through the hotel, I look in admiration and delight at the majestic interior. Amazing art lines my route, and the cool marble makes everything serene and calm. I could almost be alone because there is no one else around and once again I congratulate myself on being chosen at all.

By the time I discover the huge natural swimming pool, I am in love with this place. The pool itself looks to be carved from rock, and I adore the waterfall that spills into it from the side. It's designed to resemble a blue lagoon, and as the water sparkles, it beckons me inside like the call of the sirens.

Dropping my sarong and bag onto a luxurious white day bed, I dive straight into the crystal waters. If perfection exists, it's this place because as I leisurely swim around the lagoon, I have never been so happy. The sun shines overhead and the silence is highlighted by the fact I can hear my own breathing. There is no annoying piped music, no screaming children, no irritating people shouting and disturbing the peace, just me and every dream I ever had.

By the time I drag myself over to my day bed and lie on the soft white cushion that welcomes me to paradise, I can't keep the huge smile from my face.

After applying sunscreen, I lie back and close my eyes to sleep off the journey and just let the gentle breeze caress my body as I drift in and out of consciousness.

I suppose I must have been asleep because when I open my eyes and sit up, I'm no longer alone.

I see a couple sitting on the opposite side of the pool and look at them with interest. The woman looks to be in her late thirties and the man a little older. They are laughing with a waiter who carries a huge silver tray, loaded with more brightly coloured cocktails, and I watch them help themselves and settle back with contentment.

The waiter heads my way and smiles.

"Good afternoon, can I tempt you with a Lotus cocktail?"

"You certainly can, what's in it?" I almost can't wait to sample one and he says pleasantly, "Fresh raspberries mixed with honey, apple cider vinegar, dressed with mint leaves and topped up with cool sparkling water and crushed ice."

"That sounds amazing, thank you."

He hands me the cocktail and I say with interest. "Do you know how many people are booked in; it seems deserted?"

"After this week we are full madam. This week only invited guests are allowed, just a small group to test out the facilities."

"Lucky me."

I smile and he laughs. "Yes, lucky you."

He heads off and I sip my drink and love the sweet taste of summer. This certainly beats the rain-soaked pavements of home and I feel a little smug as I picture my friends and family back home battling with the February weather.

Sighing with contentment, I reach for my kindle and start as I mean to go on. A drink in one hand, a slushy romance in the other and the sun kissing my skin, bringing with it a healthy glow. Yes, how lucky am I?

CHAPTER 6

CHLOE

*J*ohn is already snoring beside me, and I laugh to myself. He must be exhausted. I'm tempted to give into the exhaustion myself that travelling long haul brings, but I don't want to miss a second of this.

Aside from an attractive woman lounging on the other side of the pool, we have this heavenly place to ourselves and just thinking of the week ahead makes me giddy with excitement. When the message came through that I had won this trip, I was ecstatic. Finally, some good luck for a change and I'm hoping the romantic setting and never-ending drinks will make John do something I've been waiting on for the past ten years - propose.

I steal a look at my boyfriend and hate the fact he's not my husband. When you're in your thirties and still have a boyfriend, it's a little embarrassing. The fact we have two children and a mortgage disagrees, but it's not official. It was just never the right time to splash out on the expense of a wedding and maybe this will light the romantic flame and put a rocket beneath my partner.

As I cover my body in sunscreen, I make a vow to drop

enough hints, and by the time we return to the rainy streets of home, we will have set the date.

My phone rings and when I see the screen, my heart sinks. Already; surely they should be in bed by now. Taking a deep breath, I answer it and expect the worst.

"Hey, darling, can't you sleep?"

"Mummy, why did you go? I hate gran, she made me wash up after tea, why couldn't we come too?"

Measuring my response, I say calmly, **"Because the trip was only for two, you know that, we discussed it."**

Ava, my daughter, is fourteen and at a very challenging point in her life. Nothing I say is right, and John can't even breathe near her without fear of an argument.

"What about Sasha, is she ok?"

"Who cares, she's probably sexting her boyfriend."

"Ava, don't talk like that!"

I'm shocked because even the thought of my eldest daughter having a boyfriend has seriously messed with my mind. Sasha is sixteen and at the age where she thinks she's on the shelf if she doesn't have a boyfriend. She looks more like twenty and I'm seriously worried about her because all she does is watch influencers and strive to be just like them. I'd hate to know what she does with her time and just turn a blind eye in the hope that ignorance is bliss. Usually, Ava tells me anyway as she tells tales on her sister because they don't get along. They never have.

"When are you coming home?"

Ava whines into the phone and I say slightly irritably, **"Seven days, you know that. Anyway, you should be in bed right now, not phoning me after just a few hours."**

"It's not my fault you've abandoned us. You should be here, not half way across the world. Gran just doesn't understand me like you do and she's already annoying me."

"Is she there, can I have a word?"

"No, she went to sleep hours ago, in front of the television. Then she woke up and made us go to bed, and all I can hear is her snoring from your bedroom. Honestly, mum, I'm in hell here."

Biting back a sigh, I say calmly, **"It won't be long. Why don't you call Gabby and ask her to come and meet up tomorrow, maybe go and watch a film or something?"**

"Maybe."

There's an awkward silence and I lower my voice. **"Listen, darling, I know it's difficult for you, but a week is no time at all. Just try to cope as best you can and enjoy spending time with gran. It's not as if you see her a lot these days and she loves you so much she has probably been marking the days off her calendar."**

"I suppose."

"Well, get some sleep and I'll call you tomorrow. Love you."

"Bye."

She cuts the call and John says sharply, "It's started then."

"So it would appear." Sighing, I place my phone in my bag and turn to face him. "I thought she'd at least wait until tomorrow."

"Put it on silent, she only winds you up because you let her. If she can't get through, she'll soon stop trying."

"I can't ignore her calls." I stare at him with a hint of disapproval. "She's at an impressionable age, she needs me."

"Just stop, Chloe."

"Stop what?"

"Stop pandering to her. Just cut the apron strings and let her figure it out, you're not doing her any favours."

His criticism stings, and I turn away. Despite what he says, I only do what I think is in my daughter's best interests and his constant bitching about them only makes me dislike him, and not for the first time, I feel a bitter taste in my mouth towards him. John is a good man, strong, capable and loyal. Perhaps a little too safe, but after what happened to me, it's what I need the most.

Before I met him, I had a very traumatic experience, and it's taken me a long time to get over it - if I ever have. I suppose that's why I try so hard with my own daughters, and him if I'm honest because even though he doesn't light the flame to my soul, he's everything to me and I will die trying to make this work.

Settling back, I pull on my shades and steal little glances at the lady opposite. She's an attractive woman, maybe a few years younger than us, early thirties perhaps; I'm not so sure these days. People have a habit of looking younger than they are, and part of me is jealous that she's apparently on her own. Solitary bliss, how lovely that would be. A week of alone time and sunbathing, with good looking waiters to bring me cocktails. Now that truly *is* paradise.

The sun beats down and heats my pale skin, and I seriously hope this sunscreen is up to the job. I can't remember the last time we had a break just the two of us and part of me was hoping we would be enjoying the moment in our hotel room like I'm guessing the frisky couple who fell out of the elevator are probably doing right now.

They had obviously been kissing in the lift because the woman's hair was messed up and she blushed when she saw us. I didn't miss that she adjusted her dress and the handsome man beside her smirked as we allowed them to pass.

As soon as the door closed, we heard laughter and John rolled his eyes and shook his head but I was so jealous of that woman. The man with her may have been cocky, probably due to the fact he was so handsome, and he certainly knew it. I'm lucky if we are intimate once a week these days, and I miss that first flush of love that makes everything exciting. I wonder if they're married, or on an illicit getaway.

John sits up and groans. "I'm sweating buckets here; I'm going for a dip. You coming?"

"Ok, lovely."

We head towards the pool and without waiting, John dives in and starts swimming to the other side and I sigh. Typical.

I just dip my body in and lean back, allowing the cool calm water to cleanse the heat from my body and my attention is drawn to a man on his own who has settled down on a lounger a short distance away. He looks to be in his late sixties, maybe even older, and as he looks around, he catches my eye and gives me a light smile before looking away.

The woman opposite is engrossed in her kindle and as John swims up to me, a little water splashes in my eye. "Do you know when we eat? I'm starving and just need food and my bed."

I can tell he's tired which is not surprising after the long day we've had and I shrug, "I'm not sure, I think around 7, we still have a couple of hours though, maybe you should order a snack here."

"Yeah, maybe I will and then skip the main meal." He runs his fingers through his wet hair and sighs. "You know, I think I'll do that, you don't mind, do you? I'm not sure I can wait until then, I'm dead on my feet here."

"No, it's fine, I think I'll stay up for dinner though, if you don't mind."

"Suit yourself." He heaves himself out of the pool and plods back to the sun lounger and rings the little bell on the side that every guest has.

Once again, I look at the man opposite and feel a shiver pass through me. There's something really odd about him and I can't put my finger on what it is.

CHAPTER 7

KIM

*J*ack grabs his key card and smiles as I lie in bed, reeling from the last hour. "Just off to the gym, darling."

"I don't know how you have the energy."

He winks. "I told you, holidays make me horny and now I'm keen to check out the gym."

He drops a light kiss on my cheek and whispers, "I've got a good feeling about this week."

"Me too." I stare at him with adoration and I know he loves every minute of it as he grins cockily and heads off. Feeling ungrateful, I sigh to myself. Why can't I have it all? I have most things I want, except for one thing - a family.

Seeing the family at the airport reinforced the fact I want my own so hard it hurts. If only we could have our own family, my life would be complete. Maybe this week will the best time to broach the subject. Catch him when he's relaxed and more agreeable; this could be the perfect time.

Deciding to take a cleansing shower, I allow the hot, steamy water to soothe my worries away. I could get used to this life. Thinking about the rich couple from the plane, I'm guessing this is their life 24/7 and I wonder what that feels like. To have everything and not worry about money with a husband that dotes on you and makes sure that everything is ok in your world.

Her husband was everything I want Jack to be and more. It strikes me that they don't appear to have any children. Then again, maybe they do and they were left behind, with a nanny. Mind you, that woman's figure doesn't look as if she even has food inside her, let alone a baby. No, I'm guessing she's childless, so at least we have that in common.

I wrap myself in a soft white robe and drift over to the balcony. As I lean on the edge, I gaze out at an image that I normally see on my computer screen. White sandy beach, turquoise waves, and a bright blue sky. The sun beats down on me and without thinking, I shift the robe from my shoulders, loving the way the gentle breeze caresses my heated skin.

Feeling decidedly wicked, I shrug off the robe and stretch out on the sun lounger, hoping this is as private as I think it is. It's as if I'm on the edge of paradise and I close my eyes, immersing myself in relaxation.

A gentle knock on the door makes me sit up and reach for my robe. I know Jack took the key so it can't be him, surely.

Quickly, I belt it tightly around my waist and head to open the door where I see a woman smiling from the hallway.

"I'm sorry to disturb you madam, but I have a gift for you. Compliments of the Lotus Lake Hotel and Spa."

I blink as she thrusts the biggest bouquet of lotus blooms at me that blind me with their beauty. The scent hits me almost immediately, and I stare at her in surprise as she laughs. "We want to welcome you and hope that your stay here will be unforgettable."

"Thank you, they are beautiful."

She nods. "If you need anything at all, you only have to call. My name is Chloris and I am the housekeeper."

"Thank you, um, Chloris. You are very kind."

She smiles. "Dinner is on the terrace at 7pm, I'm sure you must be hungry."

"I am, thank you."

As she leaves, I head back into the room and place the vase on the side and admire the exotic bouquet. I almost have to pinch myself because things like this don't happen to me. I'm a hairdresser from Luton and people like me don't live this life. I could get used to it, though.

Returning to my sun lounger, I stretch out in contentment and just have the delicious thought of dinner to look forward to before a cosy night's sleep in the huge emperor sized bed that we destroyed within minutes of getting here.

Thinking of my husband brings a smile to my face. How lucky am I? Jack was always the man every girl wanted. He stood out in a crowded room and drew admiring looks and wistful expressions. He was popular and certainly had his pick, but for some reason he was interested in me. He used to drop by the salon I worked in and make me laugh. Plague me for a date until I relented. Everyone warned me about what a player he was, but I was so blinded by him, I shrugged their comments aside. He was different with me. Kind, considerate and loving.

There have been a few indiscretions over the years. Once I almost left him. However, I was persuaded to give him another shot, us another shot, and I'm so glad I did because I am happy with Jack, just not complete.

Sighing, my thoughts return to the couple on the plane and I wonder what they're doing now. Probably tucking their daughters into bed right now and planning their activities for the next day. Maybe that will be Jack and me next year, I certainly hope so, and maybe this holiday is the catalyst for change. Fingers crossed, anyway.

CHAPTER 8

EVELYN

*C*harles escorted me to the spa, and that alone irritated me. It's almost as if he doesn't think I can find my own way which proves how little he thinks of me.

When I get there, he leaves and slips me the key card. "Take this, I have a meeting with Mr Wheeler to attend."

"He's here." I look at him in surprise and he nods.

"Yes, I had a text asking me to meet him in his office. He flew in this morning and has a few things to discuss. I'm not sure how long the meeting will last, so you should take this and get changed for dinner. It wouldn't surprise me if he asked us to dine with him, so be prepared for that."

"But I thought this was a holiday?"

"It is, but men like us are always working, surely you should know that better than most, darling, after all, it's what pays for your lifestyle."

"I can work."

Once again, he places his finger on my lips, effectively silencing me and whispers, "You don't need to. You just need to be beautiful and that gives me great pleasure. So, go and be beautiful, my darling, and leave the boring bit to me."

The frustration is tearing me up inside as he heads off and I feel like screaming. Be beautiful, what the hell? I am so done with him and this stupid pretty life he has all mapped out. I'm tempted to cut off my hair and turn up to dinner in a tracksuit just to show him he can't control me.

"Excuse me, madam, your masseuse is waiting."

The calm, even tones of the therapist bring me back to reality and I nod.

"Lovely, thank you."

As I follow her, I look around and note that the spa is obviously state-of-the-art because it appears that no expense has been spared. I am shown to a private room where I change into a robe and special slippers. I am instructed to lie back on a recliner and sip green tea as I fill in the usual questionnaire about my health and any allergies.

Maybe I do need to de-stress because the way I'm feeling, I'm liable to throttle my husband, so I lean back and close my eyes and try to reach my happy place, although as time goes on, I'm losing sight of where that is.

The piped music lulls me into a false state of serenity and by the time the masseuse finds me I am almost chilled.

"Follow me, madam."

She smiles pleasantly and I nod and do as she says and follow her to a darkened room and inhale the relaxing scent of jasmine and eucalyptus that fills the room. As I lie face down on the bench, she slips the robe from my shoulders and says in a whisper, "Please relax."

Closing my eyes, I give in to the moment and let her magic take effect.

Whoever this woman is, she's good at what she does because the stress just falls off me as she works her magic fingers. There is nothing but perfect solitude as she kneads my back and shoulders with sweet smelling oils as the music transports me to Utopia.

The massage lasts for thirty minutes and by the time it's over, I feel reborn. Even my anger towards Charles has dissipated and I feel very different to how I came in.

By the time I leave, I feel extremely chilled and ready for the evening ahead and make my way to the lift. As I wait, I notice the guy from the plane heading my way, dressed in shorts and a vest, with a towel wrapped around his neck. My eye is drawn to his rock-hard biceps and the sweat staining his vest, with a smattering of dark chest hair poking through that calls to the woman in me.

He stops beside me and smiles, his piercing blue eyes appraising me as they run the length of my body.

"Have you called the lift?"

He smiles and I nod. "Um, yes."

He carries on looking and I feel the heat tearing through me as he devours me with that one look alone.

"I'm Jack and I would shake your hand, but I'm guessing you would thank me not to."

He laughs softly and I join him. "Probably for the best. I'm Evelyn."

"Pretty name for a beautiful woman."

I blush and look down and luckily, the lift arrives and I hold my breath as we step inside and he leans across and presses the floor he needs, before saying, "What number?"

"Five, the top floor."

My voice sounds breathy and I mentally shout at myself. I couldn't be more obvious if I held up a banner and said, 'I want you.'

He fixes me with a molten look and says lightly, "This place is amazing, are you here for the week?"

He leans against the mirrored glass and I shift on the spot, feeling a little uncomfortable.

"Yes, are you?"

"Yes."

He doesn't even try to disguise the fact he is lusting after my body as he licks his lips and stares at my breasts. "So, lovely lady, is that your husband with you?"

"Yes, and I'm guessing you're with your wife." I raise my eyes as I stare at his wedding ring and he rolls his eyes.

"For my sins."

"Why?"

He runs his fingers through his hair. "You know what it's like, familiarity breeds contempt, and quite honestly we're hanging by a thread. I suppose this holiday came in the nick of time because we certainly need something to spice up our marriage. I'm guessing you don't have that same problem."

"No, I don't."

I glare at him but he obviously sees something different in my expression because he shifts closer and says huskily, "I saw you staring at me."

"I can assure you, I didn't."

To my surprise, he lifts his hand and strokes my face lightly and as he leans in, I feel his hot breath against my lips as he says huskily, "I saw you."

His lips are so close, one false move and they would connect with mine and I suppose it's the hint of danger, the forbidden nature of this and the recklessness that makes me lean closer and whisper, "What if I did?"

He pushes forward until my back is pressed against the wall and touches my lips lightly with his. "Maybe we should see where that attraction leads us."

My heart is beating so fast and I haven't felt this exhilarated in years. My body has been pampered and my mind is a mess because I want to kiss this man so badly it physically hurts.

The lift stops and he pulls away and as the doors open, he looks at me longingly, pressing his finger on the open button, before whispering, "What are we going to do about it?"

God knows where my sanity has gone, but I reach across and press the close button and as the lift doors shut, he reaches out and pushes me hard against the wall and smothers my lips with his. His tongue enters my mouth and I kiss him back with a fierceness that surprises me. His hand tangles in my hair and grips it hard, and he punishes my mouth in a dominant show of passion. I feel so weak with longing I almost can't breathe, and as the lift stops on my floor, I am almost tempted to drag him with me to my room. It's only the thought of Charles walking in that prevents me because I am so lost in the moment, I would agree to anything he demands.

He pulls me back inside the lift and devours my lips again and growls, "This is fate, Evelyn, do you feel it?"

I nod, my eyes so bright with passion I almost can't see straight. He whispers, "Meet me in the gym after dinner."

"I can't."

"You can."

He pushes me out and grins wickedly, saying as the door closes. "You will find a way."

As the lift disappears, I stand watching it, reeling at what I've done. What just happened? That was so unlike me, it was as if the devil danced away with my soul.

As I turn away, I feel a tingle inside as I remember his lips on mine and despite my shame, I wouldn't change a thing. That was the single most exciting thing to ever happen to me, and like a drug, I want more.

CHAPTER 9

EVELYN

*A*s soon as I get to my room, I hit the shower, desperate to erase the scent of a man from my body. What was I thinking, what have I done? Despite my shame, I feel so invigorated, alive for the first time in my life, and it's because of him. Jack.

I don't buy his story for one minute. If his marriage is hanging by a thread, mine must be dead and buried because I saw how he was with his wife. That thought alone sobers me up because of her. Thinking of the attractive woman who smiled so sweetly makes me feel ashamed. How could I kiss her husband, how could he kiss me? I'm a fool, a weak-willed idiot who let her own unhappiness drive her to the unthinkable.

Meet me after dinner. How can I? How can I not? Despite my shame and self-loathing, I want to go. I want to feel the same adrenalin rush only something forbidden can give you.

"Evelyn, darling, are you here?"

Quickly, I turn off the shower jets and wrap myself in a towel, hoping to god Charles doesn't sense something's wrong. "In here."

I call out and he opens the door and looks very pleased with himself.

"Did you have a nice time, darling?"

"Um, lovely thank you."

He nods and shrugs off his shirt and looks at himself critically in the mirror.

"I should really use the gym here; I've heard its state-of-the-art and I could certainly use some tips."

I freeze as my mind screams to me that he knows, but he just laughs and pats his imaginary stomach. "I'll sign up for a session with the personal trainer tomorrow. I've got to keep my woman interested, after all."

He turns and steps towards me and snatches the towel from my body and I stare at him in surprise. "What..."

Pulling me close, he dips his head to my neck and whispers, "I've been neglecting you. Maybe I should remedy that."

My mind is a mess as he gently nips my neck, and I hate that I feel a shiver of revulsion pass through me.

Luckily, a knock on the door interrupts his moment of passion and he sighs and pulls away. "Sorry, darling, maybe later."

He leaves me standing naked in the bathroom and closes the door softly behind him.

Grabbing the robe, I stare at my reflection in the mirror and feel so guilty I could cry. What happened in the lift was a moment of madness, something that can never be repeated, and I am so not going to meet Jack later because that will be the last time we are alone together, for all our sakes.

It takes me a few minutes to compose myself and as I head into the room, I see Charles looking at a sheaf of papers. "What are those?"

He looks up and smiles ruefully. "My homework, it would seem."

"What are you talking about?"

I feel slightly miffed and he shrugs. "The result of my meeting with Ben. He has asked me to peruse the plans of a new venture he intends on developing. I'm sorry, darling, it looks as if our plans will have to take a back seat for now."

"What plans?"

He looks mildly irritated as he stares at me with an impatient look. "Sex, darling. Isn't that where we were headed? Honestly, I sometimes wonder if you have a brain inside that head of yours."

He turns back to the papers, leaving me bristling with anger. How dare he talk to me like that, the sanctimonious beast?

His attention is now firmly on his papers and so I grab a sundress and haul it over my head and slip on my sandals, before saying angrily, "I'm going for a walk."

"Don't be long."

He doesn't even look up and I don't answer him and just slam the door on my way out, feeling the tears well up behind my eyes.

I hate him. I hate my husband and I have done for some time.

It feels so lonely being me. All around me couples get on and live their lives with laughter and shared desires. I am just an object, a plaything for my husband to pick up and put down whenever he has the time.

I wander blindly down the hallway and head for the stairs, the lift too much of a sordid memory to deal with right now.

As I head downstairs, I wonder what the answer is. Charles and I have been married for ten years. I gave up all my friends because he didn't like them and made it awkward for me to arrange dates and have them over. My family live in Spain and adore him, and the only job I ever had was working for him, which ultimately chained me to his side forever.

At first it was wildly exciting. An affair with the boss, a good looking, attentive, desirable boss. I was young and impressionable and fell completely in love with him. I thought I had it all, and I suppose I did. As the marriage progressed, I fell under his spell and did everything I could to please him. It didn't take long and I forgot who I was anymore and just became Mrs Charles Washington, the woman behind the man. Soon, I lost my mind and deferred to him in every way. He makes me feel stupid, empty headed and not worthy of heated discussion and debate. I am a pretty doll he has moulded into his perfect image of a woman. Plastic surgery, breast enhancements, you name it, he's paid for the lot and our home is no different. A show home, a place to exist, not live.

Now I've woken up and decided it's not for me, I don't know what to do about it because where will I go and how will I live? I hate that I have allowed myself to become a kept woman with no mind of her own, and I can't see a way out of this.

As soon as I reach the reception area, I spy the double doors leading to the pool. It looks so inviting I almost wish I'd worn my bikini and could take a calming dip. Maybe I would stay under the water and never resurface. That would solve all my problems – wouldn't it?

I make my way outside and worry about the direction my thoughts are heading. Have I really reached that point where death is more attractive than living? Would I seriously use that as an escape plan because to close my eyes and never wake up is looking mighty attractive right about now?

As I head into the brilliant sunshine, I feel its warm rays calming my skin and take a deep breath. I need to relax, calm my mind and work my problem through rationally, and with a maturity I appear to have lost somewhere along the way.

"Evelyn." Looking up, I see Emma waving from a sun-bed and she smiles, looking so kind I gravitate straight to her.

"Hi, Emma, this looks nice."

"It certainly is. I've had three cocktails already because a super good looking waiter keeps on feeding them to me."

She winks and gestures to the bed beside her. "If you take a seat, no doubt he'll materialise out of the shadows and bring you one."

As I position myself on the sun-bed, I look around with interest and note there are only a few other people here. "This is all a little strange, don't you think?" Emma says in a whisper.

"What is?"

"This place. It's so empty. I mean, I know we're the first guests, test pilots for want of another description, but it's almost too good to be true."

"I suppose it is."

Emma lowers her voice. "I mean, my room is seriously impressive and the welcome gift was a little over the top if you ask me."

"Welcome gift?"

"Yes, the gorgeous cocktail and note telling me to ask for anything I want. In fact, I've already drunk so much I think they're trying to lull me into an alcoholic haze for a good review."

She laughs lightly and I say enviously, "Lucky you, I don't think we had the same note."

"Oh, that's odd, maybe they'll deliver it later."

"Perhaps."

I stare at the couple across from us and Emma laughs softly. "That couple are textbook."

"What do you mean?"

46

"They are here together but hardly say two words to each other. They don't really interact, which is why I think they must have been married for a while. She's always texting, or surfing the web on her phone and he just sleeps and then dives into the pool. If they do speak, she looks annoyed, as I said, classic married life."

"You could be right."

Thinking of my own situation, I know she is and Emma says softly, "Not you though, it's obvious your husband idolises you; I've never seen a more attentive husband."

"I suppose he is."

My rings sparkle in the sunlight and Emma looks at them longingly. "You know, Evelyn, you give me hope in life."

"Me?"

"Yes, you have obviously cracked the code and if I may say so, you appear to have it all. Maybe you can tell me where I'm going wrong."

I'm spared from answering as the waiter does in fact materialise and hands me a brightly coloured cocktail.

"Madame, for you." As my fingers close around the stem, I think on Emma's words. Yes, I do have it all except for one important thing, happiness.

CHAPTER 10

CHLOE

I am so angry with myself. I've burned in the sun, despite all my best efforts, and I sigh to myself. When will I ever learn?

"That looks painful, I thought you greased up."

"I did. The sunscreen must have been out of date."

"Does that really happen?" John laughs and I stare at my reflection moodily in the mirror.

"Apparently it does."

"Never mind, it will fade by the morning and you can spend the day doing it all over again."

John sighs with pleasure as he sinks back onto the comfy bed that is better than our one at home and looks around him with satisfaction.

"You know, Chloe, I can't remember the last holiday we had where it was just the two of us."

"Me neither." I carry on applying the after sun and John says slightly irritably. "It's always been the kids. You never put me first, it's always them. Do you remember how many times I've begged you to come away with me, just the two of us, and you've always told me you couldn't leave the girls."

"What do you expect? I had them for a reason and they are best with us. Anyway, you should want to spend time with them too."

"I do, it's just that... oh, never mind."

"Spit it out, John." I feel stressed because of the state of my skin and the fact that John is always whinging about the girls seriously pisses me off.

"It's just that you never have time for me anymore. It's always the house, the girls, your job, the ironing, in fact everything except me."

"And whose fault is that?"

"Excuse me?" He looks so shocked I roll my eyes.

"It takes two to make a relationship work and all you do is go to work and expect everything done for you when you get home. It's no wonder I'm exhausted half the time. Do you think I want to do those things? I would love some alone time, a moment to myself. Someone to cook and clean for me for a change. But if I don't do it, no one else will."

"I work!"

John shouts, making me jump, and I feel the fury burning me up inside. "And I don't, I suppose."

"I didn't say that."

"What about *my* work, John? How would you like to get up before everyone else, prepare their lunches and make sure they have everything they need before they leave for the day? Plan the tea and make sure the house is presentable before heading off to the supermarket to put in a shift before coming home and cleaning the house. How do you think I feel when everyone gets home and drops their bags on the floor, raids the fridge and moans about their day before disappearing off, shouting their orders at me and leaving me to pick up after them? What about then having to cook a dinner and have everyone complain that it's not to their liking and criticise every minute that I have spent making it, before disappearing off, leaving me to once again clear up after them while they watch television and play on their iPads? How lovely to work and absolve yourself of all responsibility for just about everything else."

I turn away so he can't see the tears that are threatening to spill. Years of frustration simmering away, until one rogue comment elevates them to boiling point.

To my surprise, familiar strong arms wrap around me and pull me close and he whispers, "I'm sorry, Chloe."

I sniff and bury my face in his chest and say with muffled speech, "Thank you."

Pulling back, he looks at me with concern and wipes the tears from my eyes with his finger. "Maybe we need to set a few ground rules in place when we return."

"Such as?"

"Pull our weight a bit more. Take some of the burden from your shoulders. I can see why you have no time for me, you're too busy splitting yourself into pieces to cater for everyone. I'm guilty of that too. Maybe we should make time for each other, starting with this week. It's long overdue, anyway."

Leaning down, he kisses my lips and whispers, "Let's make this week all about you, Chloe. Let's discover each other again and where better than a tropical paradise. What do you say, babe, are you up for that?"

My smile is shaky, but my heart is full of love for this man. It always has been and I suppose we've let life get in the way of that, so I nod. "I'd like that."

He kisses my lips softly and says, "Let's head down to dinner and then turn in for the night. I don't know about you, but that flight has drained me. Tomorrow is the first day of the rest of our lives and it's all about us, Chloe and John, not mum and dad, husband or wife. It's about us as individuals and it's about time we began seeing each other that way."

I nod and feel as if a huge weight has lifted from my shoulders that I wasn't aware I was carrying. Maybe at the end of it we will have fallen in love again and finally set the date to make it official. I will certainly drop enough hints to make it happen, I just hope John listens to them.

WE HEAD down to dinner and once again I am reminded about how special this place is.

We are directed to the terrace and as I cling to John's hand, I stare in amazement at the scene before me. Tables draped in crisp white tablecloths are set before the water's edge. Fairy lights decorate the place and amazing lotus flowers bloom in crystal vases against a solitary candle. The air is full of anticipation and excitement as the other diners speak in hushed tones, as the waves lap against the shore and gentle music plays low enough to create atmosphere but not loud enough to intrude.

We are shown to a table overlooking the ocean, and the waiter says politely, "May I offer you a drink from the bar."

John catches my eye and smiles. "A bottle of champagne would be good, we are celebrating."

I look at him in surprise and the waiter smiles. "Of course. May I ask what you are celebrating?"

"Starting over."

John lifts my hand to his lips and I feel a shiver inside.

As the waiter nods and leaves, I hiss, "What are you playing at, what if the champagne is extra?"

"It wouldn't matter." John kisses my hand and smiles. "I'm going to treat you like my queen this week and hope that you will fall in love with me all over again."

"I never stopped." For a second we stare into each other's eyes and share a smile. Who knew that all it would take was

*T*he couple opposite have brought a smile to my face and Jack says with interest, "You're smiling."

Leaning in, I whisper, "The couple that just walked in are so in love, it's beautiful to see."

"Who?"

Jack turns and takes a look and shakes his head. "Oh well, it takes all sorts, I suppose."

"What do you mean?"

"Well, they're hardly in the first flush of youth, maybe this is their first holiday together and perhaps they have run away and left their husband and wife at home."

"For goodness' sake, Jack, why are you so cynical?"

He shrugs. "Years of people watching, probably."

He looks past me and whispers, "There's a couple who have it all worked out."

I follow his eye and see the glamorous couple from the plane and stare with envy at the woman's chiffon dress and silver hooped earrings. She looks immaculate and I note the perfectly manicured nails shining as she grips the stem of her wineglass. I feel quite scruffy in comparison and don't like the way Jack's gaze lingers on her just a fraction longer than necessary, although I'm having a hard time dragging my gaze from her husband, who is staring at her with adoration.

"They certainly look happy."

Jack nods. "I saw her earlier, it looked as if she came out of the spa. Maybe we should check it out, have a couple's massage or something, I think it's all included."

"Maybe." I see the cogs turning as Jack looks at the couple and I feel uneasy. I hate it when he gets that look, like he's planning something, and I wonder if he's going to sign me up for something I wouldn't enjoy. It wouldn't be the first time after all, and I'm still trying to rid myself of the nightmare when he arranged scuba diving lessons, and I almost drowned. Then there was the white water rafting we foolishly went on and when our canoe capsized, I thought my time was up. Praying to God there are no dangerous activities at this hotel, I try to distract his attention.

"I'm looking forward to a relaxing day by the pool tomorrow."

"Yes, you could use a tan, you look so pale."

"And you don't, I suppose."

I feel annoyed, and he shrugs, "That couple have tans and I'm guessing they have more than one holiday a year. I would like that for us, once a year just isn't enough."

"We don't have the money; things are hard enough without splashing out on holidays every few months."

He looks annoyed. "Maybe if you got a better job we wouldn't have to, honestly, Kim, it's not as if you're incapable and working as a hairdresser for a woman who pockets all the profits is quite sad when you think about it."

Sometimes I really loathe my husband and this is one of those times and I snap, "Well, what do you suggest I do?"

"I don't know," he shrugs. "Set up your own company,

have a bit more ambition, take charge of your life instead of sitting back and expecting me to do it for you."

"Jack!"

My voice is tight and furious. "You know why I work for Betty. I want to start a family and if I have my own business, I wouldn't have the security being employed gives me."

Jack actually rolls his eyes. "That again. Honestly, Kim, haven't you given up on that pipe dream yet? It's obvious we can't have them, so get over it."

He takes a sip of his beer and looks annoyed, and I don't miss the way his eyes are drawn to the table behind me.

Luckily, our food arrives, distracting us from a full blown domestic, and I try to enjoy the fresh lobster salad with minted new potatoes. Jack appears to be brooding about something, and a feeling of unease settles inside me that just won't go away. What's happening to us? This marriage is dissolving like an aspirin in water, and I don't know what to do about it.

After dinner, we head to the beach for a stroll and rather than holding my hand, Jack stares out to sea and I can tell something's on his mind.

"Talk to me, Jack."

"You wouldn't like what I have to say."

The fear starts to grow as I say tightly, "Tell me anyway."

Stopping, he sighs and turns to face me and I hate the pity in his eyes.

"I'm sorry, Kim, but I've been thinking for some time that maybe we need to call this a day."

I just stare at him in shock because where the hell has this come from?

He sighs and stares out at the black sea with a brooding look. "I've been unhappy for a while now; this just isn't working for me anymore."

"Since when, you were more than happy earlier, if I remember rightly."

"That was just sex, Kim, you know I'm always up for that, but outside of it, well, there's not a lot there if I'm honest."

His words strike a painful blow and I hate myself for allowing the tears to fall and turn away, not sure what to say without coming across as desperate.

He sighs heavily and says softly, "Listen, it's been a long day and I'm not thinking straight. Maybe we need a few hours apart, to think on this. We've got a week to work it out and if at the end of it I still feel the same, we will start the ball rolling when we return. It's up to you, babe, make a few life decisions and see if we can work out a way forward."

He nods to the resort. "If you don't mind, I'd like some time on my own, I'll see you back at the room."

He doesn't even look at me and just starts walking away down the beach, and I stare after him in shock. He was so cruel, so emotionless. He destroyed my world in a few sentences and made out that *he* needed time to think.

I am fast discovering the world is a lonely place when you feel as if you're the only one in it. I may be in paradise, but my soul is in hell because I have never felt pain like this. Jack wants a divorce, it's obvious. He never actually said as much, but it was there in the fine print. I have exactly one week to turn this marriage around if I want to keep him. The trouble is, right at this moment in time, I'm not sure if I do.

CHAPTER 12

EVELYN

I have been on edge all evening and it's all down to the lustful looks the man at the next table is directing my way. Charles is oblivious and just eats and drinks as if it's his last meal. The conversation is stilted because I don't have any. There is so much I want to say but know he won't appreciate hearing it.

I play with my lobster salad and resort to a few larger gulps of wine as he drones on about Mr Wheeler and how important Charles is to his business. He almost believes he owns this place as he looks around with pride and points out various things that I couldn't give a damn about.

After a while, I seize my chance when he takes a big mouthful of food and say in a whisper, "I want to have a job, Charles. I'm bored."

He almost spits out his food and stares at me through troubled eyes, and I carry on quickly before he can say no.

"I've been thinking about it for some time. I'm really interested in re-training and would love to study massage. I could work for the local spa and build up to opening my own business. It would be amazing and I would be contributing to our pot and get so much out of it. You're busy all day and I'd still be there in the evenings but to be honest, Charles, I've been thinking of this for some time and know it's the right thing to do."

He just stares at me with a horrified expression and I see the storm building in his eyes.

Regardless, I carry on laying it all out on the table. "I know you'll think I've gone mad, but I really need to do this. I've done my research and there's a course I've put my name down for. It's five days a week and would be for three months. After that I would take a position in the spa as a sort of apprentice."

"No."

He wipes the corner of his mouth with his napkin and folds it carefully, placing it neatly to the side of his plate. Then he lifts his eyes to mine and fixes me with a stern look.

"You will not be enrolling in a course and you will not work. Your job is as my wife and I expect you to fulfil your vows."

"But..." I feel the anger brewing as he leans forward and hisses. "No wife of mine is going to work, and especially not by touching another person's body. You will put all foolish notions out of your head immediately and be grateful you have the life I work hard to provide for you. Now, if you want something to do to occupy your time, I have a little project I was keeping as a surprise."

"What project?"

Like a switch, his mood shifts and he smiles smugly. "I have instructed an architect to design us a house. You can oversee the interior, which will put your talents to good use."

"A house, where?"

I stare at him in shock and he looks pleased with himself. "I have been thinking of relocating for some time now and have decided we are to move out of London to the

Cotswolds. Many people are doing that and we will have an amazing life there."

"The Cotswolds, since when?"

"Since I decided that was the best place for us. Now, darling, isn't that way more exciting that rubbing people's sweaty bodies for a living? Maybe I will even consider children. We discussed that once, do you remember?"

"And you said there was no room for children in our lives."

I stare at him in disbelief as he shrugs. "That was then, this is now."

"But I'm too old for children."

"Hardly, darling, thirty-five is a good age for children. Maybe we should start practising on this holiday."

If ever I felt trapped, it's now. As I stare at Charles in shock I see a manipulating control freak who has got worse over the years, not better. It's as if I have no say in the matter at all, and he just decides our lives with no consideration for what I want. I feel so angry I could murder him with my cutlery and happily go to prison for life because I'm there already – with him.

He looks at his watch and shakes his head.

"I need to return to the room; I have those papers to go through."

He stands, but I remain seated and he raises his eyes. "Well,"

"You go, I'm good thanks."

He looks surprised. "I can't leave you here."

"It's fine, I promised Emma I'd keep her company while you worked. She's on her own and I didn't think you'd mind."

"Emma?"

Charles looks confused. "The girl I sat with by the pool. She's really nice."

"Where is she?"

Luckily, I spy Emma sitting at a table for one trying to look inconspicuous and I wave in her direction.

"There, see."

I catch her attention and wave, and she flashes me a brilliant smile.

Charles looks put out and then sighs. "Ok, it won't hurt for an hour, I suppose. Make sure you're back by nine."

I nod as he leans in and kisses my cheek, whispering, "That's my good girl. You know I only have your best interests at heart, don't you?"

I nod as he fixes me with a dark look and I shiver inside. When did he become so sinister? I've felt it for a while now and know there's a storm building under the outward sign of composure. It strikes me that I've been a little afraid of my husband for a while now, and gradually the mask is slipping and revealing the cracks beneath. Maybe some distance is just what I need because I hate to admit it, but my husband is scaring me.

CHAPTER 13

*T*hank goodness, someone to talk to at last. It's not much fun being a single woman on holiday, and I feel self-conscious most of the time.

Evelyn sits down and looks a little shaken and I watch her husband leave and whisper, "Is everything ok?"

"Not really."

She takes a large mouthful of her wine and shakes her head sadly. "It's Charles, he is, well, he's just told me something unexpected. I'm still reeling from it."

"Do you want to talk about it?"

Shaking her head, she appears to push it to one side and says brightly, "Not really, in fact, I want to forget about Charles for a moment, I am on holiday, after all."

She looks at me with a strange hunger in her eyes. "So, tell me, how has your day been?"

"Ok, I guess."

I shrug. "I mean, this place is seriously five star, they couldn't do more for me than they have already, but it's still fairly lonely being on my own."

"You won it, didn't you?"

I nod and she says kindly, "Couldn't you find anyone to bring with you?"

"It was only for one, I would have liked the option though."

She looks interested. "Do you have a boyfriend, or husband at home then?"

"Sadly no, but I have friends who I'm sure would have been happy to accompany me."

"That's so strange because I'm looking around me and apart from that older guy over there, most people are in couples. I wonder why your invitation was only for one."

The thought had already occurred to me and I say sadly, "I expect they want to hear from a single traveller too. Maybe I'm the token single female and that guy is the male. The rest are married, or whatever they are, and they didn't need a family because it's adults only."

"Yes, that's a little strange too."

"Maybe, but it's becoming more popular now, so I believe, anyway."

Evelyn sips her drink and looks around, her gaze settling on the single man in the corner. "I wonder what his story is?"

"I'm not sure, but he was at the pool earlier. He looks nice enough and is probably glad of the break like we all are."

"Hmm." Evelyn appears distracted and I wonder about her. Outwardly, she has it all. Her husband is impressive, and she is the most well-presented woman I think I've ever met, yet there's an underlying sadness to her that I can't put my finger on.

I watch her finish her drink and then she says regretfully, "I should go. Charles told me not to be long, but I couldn't let you sit here on your own."

"You are so kind, thank you."

She stands and smiles briefly before leaving, looking a little anxious, and I wonder if Charles is as much a catch as I think because she must have only sat here for ten minutes tops.

Sighing, I raise my glass to my lips and notice the single man stand and head towards the beach. Perhaps he's going for a nice stroll to work off his meal. It wouldn't be a bad idea, but then again, I'm so tired after the flight, I really only want my bed.

I manage to hang it out for another hour before deciding to head to my room, and as I take the path through reception and wait for the lift, it strikes me how empty this place is and imagine it to be a very different story next week when it opens properly.

As I step inside the lift, I lean against the mirrored walls wearily and press for floor number 3, dreaming already of the comfortable bed waiting for me.

I must tune out for a bit because when the lift shudders to a halt and opens, I don't recognise where I am. Stepping out, I note the hallway has gone and I have walked into a large room with panoramic views of the resort.

Stepping back, I hit the steel doors and note the lift travelling back the way it came.

Quickly, I press the button and my heart rate increases because this is apparently someone's room; it's obvious by the furniture arranged around the huge open space. It's modern, luxurious and oozes wealth and good taste. Candles flicker on every surface and I hear soft music coming from hidden speakers.

Tentatively, I venture in and say loudly, "Um, is anybody here?"

There's no answer and I call again, "Hello! I'm sorry, can you help me?"

A movement by the bifold doors attracts my attention, and my heart starts beating rapidly when I see a shadowy figure watching me.

"Um, I'm sorry, I didn't mean to intrude, the lift brought me here and well, I'll just leave."

Frantically, I press the call button and then I hear, "Please, don't be afraid."

The voice has an English accent and I take a deep breath and turn, trying hard to see the man the voice belongs to because this voice is husky, deep and a little strained.

He steps into the room and I see a guy who must be around my age, although he has a beard so I can't be sure about that. He's also wearing glasses and appears well dressed in chinos and a black polo shirt. He is holding a glass of spirits in his hand and he looks at me with curiosity.

"You must have arrived today."

"I did." I swallow hard because finding myself in a room with a stranger is not what I had planned for this evening and I take a step back, willing the lift to arrive.

He looks at me with interest and says pleasantly, "How are you finding it – your stay, I mean? Are the facilities to your liking?"

"I can't fault them, it's amazing."

My voice is strained because I would give anything to get the hell out of here and he nods, apparently satisfied. "That's good to hear."

"So, um, do you live here, work here maybe?"

He laughs softly, but I fail to see the joke.

"Kind of both."

"In what way?"

He nods towards his rather oversized settee and smiles. "Would you care to join me for a drink, it would be good to hear your views on my resort?"

"Your resort." I stare at him in shock and he nods. "For my sins."

"So, it was your competition that brought me here?"

"You could say that."

"Well, um, thank you, very much actually. I couldn't believe I won."

He smiles and raises his glass and says lightly, "Please, share a drink with me…"

"Emma, um, Emma Stone, thank you."

Deciding it would be incredibly rude to refuse, I venture in tentatively, keeping my eyes on him at all times. Despite the situation I'm in, I'm curious to discover more about him and as I perch on the edge of my seat, I take the glass of liquid he offers me and wrap my hands around it tightly, desperately trying to get my breathing under control.

He sits opposite and stares at me so hard, I feel a little self-conscious. Maybe I have something on my face. God forbid it's part of that lobster I ate, that would just about sum up my life.

He stares at me thoughtfully and then he says, "I'm glad you came, maybe you will let me show you the resort personally."

As his words register, I wait for the excuses to spill from my lips because I am always so guarded but maybe it's the intoxicating setting, the fact I'm thousands of miles away from home, or the brandy he's given me but I say slightly breathlessly, "I would like that."

CHAPTER 14

KIM

*J*ack disappears into the distance and I struggle to breathe, the tears finding an outlet and streaming down my face.

He wants a divorce.

This time next week we could be calling solicitors. What will I do, how will I live without him?

For a while, I just sit on the sand listening to the waves crashing to shore and try to understand what just happened. There was no warning, no idea this was going to happen because we were happy today. Just sex, he said. I feel like such a fool as every little memory comes back to bite me.

When was the last time we talked, really talked? How many times has he sat apart from me on planes? He always has an excuse not to talk. There's the television at home, the programme he wants to watch, the email he must reply to. The phone calls and the need to get an early night. It's only now I realise Jack hasn't tried for some time and I wonder if he's hiding something. Maybe it's because I push him to start a family. Perhaps he has the inability to do so and can't bring himself to tell me. I can't believe he doesn't want a family, surely everyone does.

My tears dry as I think more about the reasons why he's dropped this bombshell on the first night of our holiday. What good does it achieve? We have seven days together. Why break up now?

The more I think about it, the more I doubt his reasons. There's something troubling him, and I have exactly seven days to discover what that is.

Sadly, I retrace my footsteps along the beach and head for the hotel. I can see my fellow guests enjoying an after-dinner drink on the terrace and divert my route around them through the trees. I don't want to face anyone and certainly not see how happy they all are. I'll just head back to the room and wait for him. Maybe he will regret this, then again…

Sighing, I am so deeply wrapped in my thoughts, I don't think about the route I have taken and a rustling in the bushes makes my heart skip a beat. I quicken my pace hoping it's just an animal, but the rustling follows me and I feel sick. Someone's there, in the bushes and they are following me.

I don't know why, but it's as if I know something bad is going to happen. It's a sixth sense, something I've had a few times before, and I was always right. So, I start to run, stumbling a little as I go, and I stifle a sob as the sound travels with me.

By now I am running and only the bright lights of the hotel guide me because I'm in the shadows and I berate myself for being so damned stupid.

I risk a look behind me but see nothing, and as I turn to the front, I run into a hard body and scream.

A hand clamps over my mouth and a firm voice says, "It's ok, you're safe, what is it?"

Looking up, I see the smart gentleman from the plane and

I gasp, "Oh thank god, I think someone's in those bushes and they're following me."

He looks past me and frowns. "Wait there."

"But…"

"It's fine, if there is someone there, I'll flush them out."

He marches toward the bush and calls loudly, "I know you're in there, come out and show yourself."

The only sound is my heavy breathing and the distant call of a nocturnal creature.

He heads back and shakes his head. "You shouldn't be out here alone, anything could happen."

"I'm sorry." I stare at him meekly and he says with concern.

"You've had a shock, come, I'll take you inside, find you a brandy, or your husband if you prefer." He smiles and I shake my head and shiver. "The brandy sounds good; I doubt my husband would care, anyway."

Once again fresh tears fall and he looks concerned.

"Don't worry, I'll make sure you're safe."

He takes my arm and pulls me along with him, and it strikes me how kind he is. Nothing like Jack, just a kind man helping a stranger.

We head inside and he guides me towards the bar and says loudly, "Two brandies please."

The bartender nods and before long we have hold of them and I proceed to empty the glass in one go.

He smiles and says to the bartender. "Another one I think and make it a double this time."

We take a seat on two bar stools and he looks at me with concern. "There, that must feel better."

"Thank you, it does."

I smile shyly and notice how attractive he is close up. More than I thought, and there is something nice about having him by my side.

"So, what made you go for a lonesome walk on the beach?" He looks concerned and I sigh heavily. "I wasn't alone – at first, anyway."

"What happened?"

He looks confused and I say sadly, "My husband dropped a bit of a bombshell on me and left."

"The resort?"

"No, just me." Once again, the tears build and I try to blink them away as he frowns. "So, let me get this straight. Your husband left you abandoned alone on the beach in the pitch black in a foreign country."

"Yes." I try not to look at him and he shakes his head. "Whatever his reasons, he should be strung up. What sort of man does that to a lady, especially his lady?"

"He was angry."

"No excuse." He seems genuinely annoyed and once again I feel a surge of jealously for his glamorous wife. She doesn't know how lucky she is to have a man like that by her side.

He smiles gently. "So, what will you do now?"

"Go back to the room and wait for him I suppose."

"Hmm, maybe you shouldn't."

"Why not?"

He grins. "Make him worry for a bit. In fact, make him worry a lot."

"How?"

"There's a movie running in the cinema suite, it's one I fancy watching, why don't you join me?"

"But your wife, won't she miss you?"

A flash of bitterness passes across his face as he says tightly, "I doubt it. She will be too busy with her new-found friend to care. They are probably drinking themselves sense-less as we speak."

"Her friend?"

"A woman she met by the pool. Maybe we should both

remind our spouses of their loyalties. So, what do you say, would you like to share some popcorn with me?"

He reaches out and takes my hand and as he helps me from my stool, I feel a shiver of excitement pass through me. This is unexpected but nice. Nice to do something different, with someone different, and the icing on the cake will be if Jack returns and finds me missing. Maybe he will think twice about his conversation when he thinks I've gone.

CHAPTER 15

EVELYN

*A*gainst every warning siren in my head, I find myself hovering outside the gym. It's so silent here, there is nobody around and only my rapid heartbeat to keep me company.

I am so nervous I jump at the slightest sound, and yet there's a sense of anticipation building that sets me on fire. I'm loving this. The thrill of not knowing what's going to happen. The forbidden element, the sense of doing something wrong. It's like a huge shot of adrenalin that I badly need in my life, and I wonder what Charles would say if he knew of my intentions.

I hear footsteps approaching and my heart rate increases and I daren't turn around. This is it; I'm really going to do this and as a hand wraps around my eyes, I am pulled against a hard body and hear a husky, "Good girl."

My heart flutters as he begins to kiss my neck and I gasp as a delicious shiver runs through me. He nips at my skin and as I moan, he whispers, "In here."

I find myself thrust into a darkened room that can only

be described as a large cupboard and before I know it, my dress is ripped off and I am pushed facing the wall. I hear a zipper and start to shake as he stands behind me and growls, "You are one naughty girl."

As he thrusts inside, I briefly tense because something about this feels so wrong and dirty, and yet I'm loving every minute as he pushes into me and strips me of every principle I own.

The fact it's pitch black only adds to the excitement. It almost makes it acceptable because I can't see the man I shouldn't have. Another woman's husband, a stranger but a man I want more than I want my morality it seems.

Sex with Jack is so different. So exciting, compelling even, and I almost welcome the fact he strips away any dignity I have and ruins me forever.

It's such a confined space which makes the heat build and feeling him hard inside me makes me lose my mind. I love this, the danger, and the fact it's so wrong, is turning me on way more than I thought. I don't even think about our partners who are probably wondering where we are. For now I'm enjoying a moment that's just for me. Something Charles can't control; emancipation from a marriage I feel trapped in. This is all about me and what I want. What I do with my body, my own choice, and I become a little wild as I give him back as good as he gives me.

Sex with Jack is exhilirating, slightly dirty and passionate, nothing like the usual act of going through the motions with Charles. Now I know what all the fuss is about as I feel the orgasm tearing through me as I crave even more.

He clamps his hand around my mouth as I scream in ecstasy. Then before I've even recovered, I hear the door slam behind me, leaving me a quivering, lust filled, dirty mess.

~

THE WALK of shame is an interesting one because after doing my best to clean myself up, I edge the door open a crack to check that the coast is clear.

As I dust myself down, I feel like a wicked woman as I start a slow walk back to my room. Despite everything, I would do it again; I hope to do it again because this is the last shred of control I have. The one thing Charles can't own - my body.

Now I've sampled the freedom it gives me; I like it and I'm already planning my next encounter. It feels so good, so forbidden and so wrong, and I don't even spare a thought for Jack's wife.

She gets him all the time, let someone else have the pleasure for once. I'm not sure how I've forgotten to bring my morals with me, but it's as if the usual rules don't apply here. I mean, he said himself, their marriage is hanging by a thread, possibly over. I can relate to that, so what's the harm in colouring outside the edges from time to time.

I'm almost afraid to go back to my room because I'm certain Charles will be there, waiting with a disapproving stare as he demands to know where I've been. Therefore, I'm surprised to find it empty and feel the relief hit me as I race to the shower before he returns.

As I look at my reflection in the mirror, I thank god he wasn't here because it's obvious what I've been doing. My hair is a mess and my lips swollen. There's a slight bruise around my neck and I shiver when I remember how rough he was. I loved it, every minute because there was more passion in that encounter than there has been in the past ten years with Charles.

I don't regret a moment of what we did because I needed

it like a drug. It gave me a shot of life when I thought I was dying. A hunger for more and a desire for freedom that I have kept firmly buried inside. Maybe I needed this trip to shock me into life again because now I've had a taste of forbidden fruit, I'm hungry for more.

CHAPTER 16

CHLOE

*T*he moonlight dances on the waves that gently lap to the shore and I feel at peace with myself. As I hold John's hand, I shiver with anticipation. I never thought for one moment we would be enjoying this all-expenses holiday in February. We haven't had a holiday for years, there was never enough money to waste, and now I see what was missing. We need this time to reconnect as a couple and make some time for us.

I am distracted by a figure of a man walking slowly up the beach and peer into the darkness. He's too far away to make out his features, and strangely I feel annoyed that he is here at all.

John raises my hand to his lips and whispers, "This is nice."

"It is."

I love the way he wraps his arm around me and pulls me close as we study the inky black sea and listen to the sound of nature. I'm not even cold because even though the heat of the sun has faded, there is only a balmy breeze to take its place.

"We should do this more often." John voices my own thoughts and I nod. "We should."

The man passes and now all I can see is his silhouette walking back to the resort and I am literally glad to see the back of him.

Impetuously, I reach up and drag John's lips to mine and kiss him softly and with so much love, it feels as if this is our first kiss. It's different here, romantic, magical, and has more feeling than the perfunctory ones we enjoy at home before he turns his back on me and falls asleep. Even sex is carried out in the darkness, once a week behind a locked door. Any noise is muffled because the girl's bedrooms are a stone's throw away and the thought of them hearing us is not a pleasant one.

Here we are free. We have a week to rediscover our connection and I feel excited for that.

John pulls back and his voice is husky as he whispers, "Shall we go to bed?"

"I thought you'd never ask."

I giggle as he growls and pulls me along after him and like a couple of teenagers, we race back up the sand towards the resort.

As we spill through the double doors, the receptionist calls out, "Excuse me."

John groans, "What now?"

We head across and the woman smiles. "I trust you're enjoying your stay."

"Lovely, thank you."

She smiles. "I'm sorry to interrupt your evening, but I have you down on the list to take the boat to Kurraga town tomorrow."

We look at one another in surprise.

"Did you book that?" I stare at John in surprise and he shakes his head. "No."

The receptionist smiles. "It's one of the complimentary excursions all the guests are signed up for. We would like your feedback on the experience and I'm sorry, but seven days just isn't nearly enough time to pack it all in."

I nod, but inside I feel a little annoyed. I really wanted to lie by the pool, although my skin may be dancing for joy at the thought of some respite from the sun, but I just smile gratefully. "That sounds amazing, what time?"

"It leaves at 9am, which should give you time to enjoy breakfast before meeting the rest of your party on the jetty."

John nods and says impatiently, "Thank you."

He turns to go, and the receptionist says quickly, "Enjoy your evening and don't forget to report any problems with your room."

John practically drags me away and mumbles, "Great, a morning shopping instead of sleeping by the pool. If I had known we would be signed up for everything going, I wouldn't have come."

I feel a little hurt at his words and yet I shrug it off because I'm guessing he's just annoyed his day has been planned for him. Of course, he would have come and only a fool would remain in England when paradise beckons.

We head to the lift and I notice the single man from the pool waiting and something about him makes the hairs on my neck stand to attention. I'm not sure why, but he has a look about him that gives me the creeps and I stand a little behind John and hear him say in a deep voice, "Good evening."

Luckily, John answers for us both and thankfully the lift arrives and as we crowd into the space, John politely asks him which floor.

"Three please."

It's a little awkward as we ride the lift in silence, and there's a prickle of tension running down my spine. Something that makes me raise my guard a little and try to look invisible.

I'm not sure why I'm so on edge. After all, this man is a stranger to me, but there is something there, something odd about him and I can't put my finger on it. When you know something's not quite right but don't know what it is, the air around you changes and I feel that now. When he steps outside, it's as if I can breathe again and I haven't had this feeling for quite some time, which tells me there's a storm building in paradise.

CHAPTER 17

EMMA

a gentle tap on my door wakes me around 8am and as the sun filters through the cracks in the blind, it takes me a moment to remember where I am. Then it hits me and I stretch out with contentment as I remember – I'm in paradise.

The tap gets louder and I drag myself from the warm, cosy bed and head to the door. I open it a crack and see a uniformed waiter standing beside a trolley, and he nods respectfully. "Room service."

"But I didn't order this."

I stare at him in surprise and he smiles. "Compliments of the hotel, madam. Breakfast on your balcony."

"Wow, thank you." I open the door a little wider and as he wheels the trolley inside, I actually pinch myself. Surely, I'm still dreaming because things like this don't happen to an ordinary girl like me.

As the waiter sets up the breakfast trolley on the balcony, I watch him arranging the silver dishes filled with hot scrambled eggs and bacon. Fresh fruit and natural yoghurt nestle beside a bread basket of pastries still warm from the oven.

Freshly squeezed juice of every variety in little glass jugs sit beside crystal glasses and a selection of conserves look tempting accessed by way of a small silver spoon in every pot.

He finishes up and nods respectfully. "Tea and coffee are on the lower shelf with your choice of cream or milk. Please call if there are any special requirements, such as an omelette or pancakes. The smoked salmon is also a favourite, so please make sure to call if you prefer that."

"Thank you so much." Quickly, I grab my purse and remove a few notes and yet as I offer him the tip, he shakes his head. "No need, madam, your stay here is complimentary and that included any tips."

"But…"

"Good day, madam. The maid will sort out your trolley when she makes up your room later. If you need it collecting beforehand, please call 505."

He turns to leave and I stare after him in surprise. This is unimaginable luxury. Breakfast on the balcony. I don't even have to get dressed and can just relax and read my kindle while I enjoy the ultimate in relaxation.

As I approach the trolley, I see an envelope propped up in the middle. My heart beats a little faster for some reason as I draw out a thick cream card and note the spidery hand-writing.

Good morning Emma, I would be honoured to show you around the resort today. I will call for you at 10.30am.

Ben X

Wow, a date with the owner. This is above the five-star rating. It's like being invited to dinner with the Captain on a cruise ship. My own personal guided tour with the man in charge.

As I help myself to breakfast, I think about the man I met last night. Ordinarily, I don't go for men with beards or glasses, but there was something about that man that felt safe. He was a little intense, but in a good way. I didn't miss the way he stared at me – hard, for most of the hour I spent in his company. His dark hair and immaculate clothes impressed me, as did his apartment that was even more luxurious than this president's suite. He listened to every word I said as if he needed to know so badly every thought in my head. It was quite an intense experience, and it was only when I reached my room, that the daze I was in left me.

Just thinking of seeing him again brings with it an excitement that is making my stay here even more intoxicating and as I settle down to eat, my kindle is forgotten as I stare out to sea and wonder how I got so lucky.

10.30 BRINGS a knock to my door that makes me jump and sends a shiver down my spine.

He's here.

Smoothing down my simple sundress and fixing my sunglasses firmly on top of my head, I grab my bag.

I open the door and catch my breath because he is standing waiting, looking so incredibly gorgeous in a white t-shirt and khaki cargo shorts. He is wearing leather flip flops and I note an expensive Rolex on his wrist and am pleased to see there is no wedding ring.

His eyes rake my body appreciatively and he holds out his hand.

"You look lovely, Emma, come, there's a lot to see."

Why I grasp his hand so readily is a surprise to me because surely that's a little presumptuous, and as his hand closes around mine, I feel a shiver of expectation. He's interested in me, Emma Stone, single and desperate to mingle and what a catch to land.

We head towards the lift and he says in a deep voice, "I trust you enjoyed your breakfast."

"It was lovely, thank you."

"I thought you would prefer to eat in your room because I'm guessing it's not much fun eating alone."

"You are so thoughtful."

He nods, and it strikes me how serious he is. "I like to take care of my guests."

"Well, you've certainly done that. Is this service going to be standard because I've never known anything like it?"

He shakes his head. "A scaled-down version, but I pride myself on excellence, I always have."

We step into the lift and for some reason it feels more intimate in here, probably because he is standing so close to me, his fingers holding onto mine tightly. He looks at me and just stares and if anything, I feel a little uncomfortable and say quickly, "From your accent you're British, how did you end up here?"

"I didn't."

He smiles. "My business is in London; this is just one of my investments. I have several others that require my time, but for obvious reasons I needed to be here this week."

Thinking about the launch, I nod. "Yes, I suppose it's a very exciting time for you."

"It is – very."

Part of me wonders if he's referring to his business or something else because his voice has an edge to it that tells me something more is going on in his mind.

The lift arrives and we step outside into the brightly lit reception and he pulls me along by his side at a rapid pace.

For most of the morning, he shows me paradise. From the sumptuous pool that I visited yesterday, to the gym, spa and tennis courts. There are two more pools and several hot tubs, not to mention the beautiful white beach that appears to stretch for miles with no other building in sight.

He leads me down a wooden jetty towards a beautiful motor cruiser where a man in uniform is waiting.

"Good morning, sir."

The man nods and Ben stops and says gently, "Allow me to show you the rest of the Island."

"On here?"

He laughs at my expression. "Yes, The Lotus is my pride and joy and has every luxury I could cram into the space. So, what do you think, it's a beautiful day to explore?"

I don't need asking twice and follow him on board and take a brightly coloured cocktail that another steward hands me from a silver tray.

Ben slips his arm around my waist and guides me to the front of the boat and as the engines start, we sip our drinks, looking out on a beautiful turquoise sea.

CHAPTER 18

KIM

*I*t feels a little awkward standing, waiting for the boat to Kurraga. Jack was sleeping when I got in and hasn't said two words to me today. Breakfast was conducted in silence and I can tell he's angry. The fact he hasn't even bothered to ask me where I was, shows how little he cares and I am so angry right now. I don't deserve this, he's a cruel, nasty man and after spending a very pleasant evening with Charles, it just reinforced the fact that I married a brute.

We stand watching the other guests arrive and I steal glances at Charles and his wife Evelyn. He catches my eye on a couple of occasions and the look he gives me makes me feel warm inside. He was so attentive last night. Kind, funny, charming and courteous. I didn't feel the least bit uncomfortable around him and once again I envy his wife her husband.

The boat arrives and I watch the nice couple giggling as she steps on board and stumbles and I love the way her husband reaches out to steady her. It's obvious they are happy, unlike us, and dare I say it, Charles and Evelyn.

The usually cool, chic woman, looks a little worse for

wear today. She is wearing her large sunglasses, but her shoulders sag a little and she seems on edge.

He is holding her against his side protectively and I wonder if she has a drink problem. She is certainly a little unsteady on her feet, and he helps her on the boat and throws me a small smile when Jack isn't looking.

Jack also seems on edge, and I can tell he's angry. Well, that's nothing to how I'm feeling because he has created this atmosphere, not me. I thought we were set for a romantic break and after the first few hours spent in bed, I assumed we were starting as we meant to go on.

An overwhelming feeling of sadness grips me as I think about my husband and our deteriorating relationship. I'm doubtful if there's a way back for us, especially after Charles showed me what a proper gentleman behaves like.

The last passenger is a man on his own and I'm not sure why, but I dislike him on sight. He is staring at me when he thinks no one is looking, and I don't like the expression in his eye. There is something about that man that makes my flesh creep and I wonder what his story is? Not that I intend on finding out, because the least time I spend with him, the better.

Jack looks out across the water broodingly, as the boat starts and I wonder if we are actually going to speak at all today. Once again, I look across at Charles and find him watching me and I throw him a small smile.

He returns it and a warm feeling spreads through me because there's a man I would really like to get to know.

Despite the company, we dock at the local town and I look around me with interest. It's so pretty with its brightly painted wooden houses that double as shops, their locally made treasures spilling from them in a collective burst of colour.

The other passengers disembark and I hear Charles say

loudly, "Come on, darling, I'm sure there are a few shops here who would welcome the economic boost your visit will give them."

He guides her away from the rest of us and if anything, she looks as if she could use a good sleep rather than a day spent trawling around the local town.

The nice couple hold hands and disappear up the street, and I'm glad to see the man heading in the opposite direction.

Jack hunches his shoulders and says in a bored voice. "This is just great. Why on earth did we agree to this in the first place?"

"Because we owe it to them. They have paid for our trip, so the least we can do is sample their excursions and give our honest feedback."

Deciding to make the best of a bad situation, I say with resignation, "Come on, let's just explore the town, there may be a nice bistro or bar we can set up camp in. We've only got three hours, anyway."

He nods, and we set off, an awkward silence settling between us.

All around us are people enjoying the sunshine and laughing as they take photographs on their phones. The only thing we're doing is walking under a cloud and I decide that I've had enough and say tentatively, "We really need to talk, this silence isn't doing either of us any favours."

"First, tell me where you went last night." He looks at me with a fierce expression and I hide a small smile. Maybe he was jealous, possibly testing me and hoping I would be waiting for him. Maybe he was about to apologise and say he didn't mean it. I'm not sure what I think about that and just shrug.

"I went for a walk, a long one."

"Do you really expect me to believe that? You were trying to get back at me."

"No, Jack, I was trying to make sense of what you said to me. It's not every day my husband tells me he's calling time on our marriage. I was shocked, upset and a little bit devastated in case you were wondering."

Turning away, I pretend to be interested in a shop display of brightly coloured scarves, and he stands moodily beside me.

Then he says in a softer voice, "If it's any consolation, I was upset too."

"Really."

I don't look at him and he snatches hold of my hand and says roughly, "Look at me."

Turning my eyes to his, I see a myriad of emotions swirling in his eyes and his voice is gruff as he whispers, "I hated doing that. To be honest, I'm not sure why it came out the way it did. It was as if I had no control over my words. I suppose it's been festering for a few months now and well, perhaps I had too much to drink and got a bit carried away."

"What are you saying?" I genuinely don't know, and he shrugs. "I don't want to fall out with you, Kim, you mean too much to me for that, it's just, well… it's just that I don't think I love you anymore."

My lip trembles as I see the genuine remorse in his eyes. This is harder to bear than his angry words of yesterday. This time it's considered and well thought out after a night's sleep, and I guess this tells me my answer.

Turning away, I say tightly, "Then there's nothing more to say. As soon as we return to the hotel, I'll make arrangements for my own room. Cut our losses and set the wheels in motion to go our separate ways."

If I thought my words would shock him, it doesn't work because he just nods. "Probably for the best. Anyway, if you don't mind, I think I'll find a bar somewhere to be alone. Enjoy your shopping."

He drops my hand and turns his back on me, and I stare after him in total shock. Our marriage crumbles and he tells me to enjoy my shopping. Is he mad, deluded, a fool?

Fighting back the tears, I realise that I'm the fool, not him. I should have seen this coming because if I'm honest, the writing's been on the wall for several years now. So, that's it, no marriage and no family because the chances of me finding a man who wants a family at this point in my life, are about as certain as winning the euromillions.

CHAPTER 19

CHLOE

*T*his is so lovely; the small town is quirky, and I love the colourful buildings and general festive vibe. John and I made love this morning while the sun kissed our bodies through the open bifold doors. We were served breakfast in our room and are now looking forward to a complimentary excursion to the nearby town to take advantage of local culture and discover a place I never knew existed until today.

We wander through a street market hand in hand and I am happier than I have ever been. Even my morning call from Ava didn't dampen my mood, even when she told me her sister was out with her new boyfriend as we speak.

John groans. "Hey, Chlo, I really need to use the toilet, do you know where they are?"

"No, but there's a bar across the road. We could grab a drink there."

"Great."

We head towards a lovely little bar nestling on the pavement and as I take a seat, John heads inside.

It feels so good to be out and free. No miserable, dreary

weather to dampen my spirits. No cleaning, cooking or general stuff to burden me down. Just pure enjoyment on tap 24/7 and if I could change one thing, it would be to make our stay two weeks instead of one.

"Excuse me."

I blink and looking up, see the man from the boat and my nerves start prickling as I say quickly, "Oh, hi."

He drags one of the chairs beside me and stares at me long and hard. "I recognised you from the resort, I'm Sam by the way."

He holds out his hand and I hate the fact I must shake it and say quickly, "Um, Chloe and my husband's John."

For some reason I don't want to label John as anything else because I sense there is something dangerous about this man.

He doesn't appear in any hurry to release my hand and I pull it away awkwardly, praying that John will charge out and rescue me. I look towards the bar with a hopeful expression, but there's no sign of him.

"So, are you enjoying your stay?" His husky voice sets my teeth on edge and I force a smile on my face.

"It's lovely, are you?"

"Yes, although it's getting a little lonely already."

"Didn't you have anyone you could bring with you?"

"No, sadly I'm on my own."

He stares at me with an intense look and says creepily, "All the good ones are already taken."

I feel uncomfortable as he undresses me with his eyes and I shift a little on my seat.

"Oh, well, never mind, I'm sure the right woman is just around the corner."

"You could be right."

He smiles, and it makes me feel dirty because he is staring at my breasts and not into my eyes. In fact, his gaze travels the length of me as if he's appraising a horse and I say tightly, "So, anyway, where are you off to now? I heard there's an amazing aquarium not far away."

He says nothing and just continues to look me up and down and then he slips a piece of plastic towards me and winks. "My key card for room 360, if you get bored with your husband come and find me."

I stare at him in shock and drop the card as if it burns. "How dare you?"

He just laughs at the disgust on my face and leans in. "Women like you love it. I've seen your little looks my way, dreaming of me and what I can give you. Your husband just isn't good enough, boring, safe and disinterested. Well, you only have to say the word and I'll give you more excitement than you ever dreamed of. So, before you get those tight knickers in a twist, think about it."

He winks and pushes away from the table and then luckily heads off before I can answer him. I can't stop shaking as I stare down at the table, feeling so dirty inside. It feels as if an unwanted virus is creeping through my body, replacing good with evil and happiness with terror.

I try so hard to fight it but the memory is there - always there, lurking in the deep recesses of my soul, waiting for an opportunity to re-surface and destroy me all over again.

Twenty-two years earlier.

The music is so loud, deafening even, and I feel a little unsteady on my feet. My friends are loud tonight, in fact everything is loud.

Anna yells in my ear, "Come and dance, Chloe."

I feel a little nauseous and shake my head. "Sorry, I feel strange, I should go somewhere quiet for a minute, maybe sit down."

"You ok, babe?" The soothing voice of Alice, the sensible one among us, cuts through the fog in my brain and I muster up a smile. "I'll be fine, you go, have a dance for me."

She looks at me with concern as Anna whines, "I love this song, it's my favourite and that guy I've got my eye on is sending me the vibes."

"But..." Alice looks worried and I say firmly, "Go, I'll just grab a glass of water and sit down for a while."

Anna drags her off and I'm glad about it because I'm struggling to stand, let alone dance, and so I quickly head to the bar to grab a glass of water. My heart sinks when I see the crowd filling the bar four deep and I turn away.

I must have eaten something because I was fine an hour ago. Mum's shepherd's pie must have been past its sell by date because that's all I can taste and I know it's going to make an appearance again very soon.

I decide to head to the toilets and see if I can splash some water on my face because I am sweating so much and it's not just because it's so hot in here.

As I stumble through the club, I try to dodge the crowds but it's almost impossible and I knock a few drinks on my way and hear lots of complaints.

As I reach the door leading to the toilets, I stumble through, grateful for the sound being shut out by the large heavy door.

Luckily, it's quieter out here and I make my way to the ladies, praying there's not a queue because I'm not sure if I will make it at all.

I almost make it before a firm hand grabs my elbow and says in a deep voice, "Are you ok?"

"Not really." My legs almost give way and he says with authority, "Let me help you."

Feeling grateful for any kind of help, I nod and allow him to propel me towards another door and guess he must work here. Maybe they have a first aid room and I can lie down and gather my sanity, and as he propels me through the door, the cool air hits me as if it's the cure for everything. Taking a few deep breaths, I blink and look around me and see we have left the club and are in an alley outside. I make to turn around and suddenly find myself *pushed hard against the wall and as my face meets it, he stands behind me and growls, "Is this what you want, you're all the same, teasing men with your short skirts and sexy moves."*

I try to fight but he's too strong and to my horror, I feel him lift my skirt and press into me. As I open my mouth to scream, it all goes blank and I know nothing of the horrors he inflicts on me because when I next wake up, I'm lying in a hospital bed with my mum crying bitterly beside me.

"Hey, penny for your thoughts." I open my eyes and see John looking at me with concern across the table, and I shake away the memory.

"I'm good. Sorry, I must have drifted off there for a second."

"What were you thinking?"

"Nothing, you know - the girls - are they ok, that sort of thing."

"I wouldn't worry, I mean, you only spoke to them about an hour ago, you must stop worrying."

He settles back and grabs the menu and I nod and do the same, but I don't see the words. Stop worrying, how can I? I have two daughters for god's sake and just thinking of them ever being in the same position that I was, makes my heart scream with pain.

What happened that night will haunt me to my dying day because I never recovered from the whole sordid experience. The man was never caught, and I had to endure the humiliation of police questioning and my parent's devastated faces every time they looked at me. It turns out he slipped something in my drink and followed me out. Date rape they called it; I never did. A brutal assault was more like it and the memory catches me when I least expect it and that man has brought it back to the surface in a devastating way.

His key card mocks me from the table and I swallow the

fear. I should tell John, tell the hotel owner; I should make it known there's a predator among us, but my heart sinks when I realise I won't. I can't even form the words because I can't revisit a subject I have locked deep down in a box inside my soul because if I let it out, it would destroy everything I have worked so hard to forget.

CHAPTER 20

*C*harles knows something. His manner has changed since yesterday. He is dismissive, crueller than usual, and can't look me in the eye.

He wasn't here when I got back around 11pm. I was so nervous and had my excuse ready should I need to explain my whereabouts. I didn't need it. He returned around midnight and just changed and curled up in bed beside me, turning the other way.

I think I died a thousand times during the night from pure terror. I couldn't sleep and just lie stiff and full of shame after an evening spent doing something so wrong, I doubt I'll ever recover.

I am certain he knows because why else would he be so cold?

This trip is the last thing I need today because I can hardly stand, let alone walk through the hot streets of Kurraga. To make matters worse, we appear to be following Jack's wife around because every shop we stop at she's already there.

Luckily, there's no sign of Jack and I wonder why? I can

tell she's upset, it's obvious by the way she looks blindly around her and just pretends to focus on the products on sale, but I can tell she's staring at nothing, really.

Maybe Jack told her, perhaps she confronted him and he confessed. Just thinking of anyone finding out fills me with anxiety and I can't even look at him today because of what we did.

I am going to Hell because I have committed the ultimate betrayal against my husband and against a woman who doesn't deserve this treatment.

However, I can't contain the delicious shiver that passes through me when I think back on the whole experience. Jack was everything I hoped he'd be. Strong, passionate and sexy. A man full of passion who isn't afraid to reach out and take what he wants. A man I am fast realising I prefer over one who treats me more like an object than a living, breathing, human being with feelings.

I try anything to create distance between us and armed with a heap of clothes to try on, head for the nearest changing room. Charles waits patiently outside and I intend on taking my time, but all I do is sit on a chair with my head in my hands. How has my life fallen apart so quickly? I knew I had fallen out of love with Charles a while ago, but I've never been a woman who cheats. I've had countless offers but always resisted, which is why what happened last night is so shocking. Thinking of Jack, I get the flutters because if I could run away with him and never face Charles again, I would. But he's created distance from me, and his wife it seems, and I wonder where he is.

I suppose twenty minutes is pushing it slightly and I grab the clothes and head outside, not having tried one item on.

Charles is chatting to Jack's wife and my heart sinks and I'm sure my guilt must be written all over my face as he beckons me over and says with a wicked grin that worries me still further, "Have you met Kim, Evelyn?"

She smiles, but I notice the tremble to her lips and I feel like the biggest bitch in the world.

"Hi." My voice sounds strained and I can't look her in the eye and Charles frowns, saying gruffly, "Any good?"

"I'm sorry, what?"

He sounds impatient, "The clothes, do you want them?"

Noticing the hopeful smile on the shop assistant's face, I nod and thrust them towards him. "Yes, I'll take them all."

"I thought you might."

He shakes his head and tosses them on the counter and turns to Kim. "Are you here alone, I thought I saw your husband with you?"

I almost miss it, but I see a look pass between them and Charles looks concerned. Kim just looks at him and sighs. "He's exploring on his own."

Charles nods and I think my life flashes before my eyes when he turns to me and says sharply, "Evelyn, why don't you go with Kim and grab a table at the café I saw across the street while I pay for these. Order a bottle of red and white, unless Kim prefers something different. I won't be long."

Kim shakes her head, looking nervous, "Oh, I couldn't intrude, it's fine…"

"Nonsense, I will not have you walking around a strange place on your own, not on my watch."

Kim smiles at him gratefully and I sigh inside; could this day get any worse?"

Trying to do the right thing, I smile.

"Come on, I'm desperate for a drink, anyway."

"Hmm." Charles throws me an acid look. "So I gathered after last night."

Turning my back on him, I leave the shop with Kim in tow and feel so embarrassed I can't even look at her. Kim almost has to run to keep up with me and says apologetically, "I'm so sorry, I could just slip away. Tell him that Jack came back. You really don't have to…"

"It's fine." My tone is curt and I sigh heavily and turn to face her with an apologetic smile. "Listen, I'm sorry, I didn't mean to sound so rude. It's just that, well, you know how it is with married couples, we're winding each other up and it's not going to end well."

"Same." She seems so sad I hold my breath and wonder whether to ask or not. Any normal woman would, but I would feel like a hypocrite if she offloaded her troubles onto me, the woman who is probably responsible for them in the first place.

"Are you ok, do you want to talk?" The compassionate woman in me speaks up and I almost dread her answer. She appears to shake herself and says with a smile, "I'm fine, thank you, just a little too much sun, probably."

We grab a seat in the sweet little bar across the street and as we sit down, I feel glad to be under a canopy and out of the sun. Fanning myself, I say with a groan, "I would rather be sunning myself by the pool. This was a seriously bad idea."

"Yes, it is rather hot." She smiles and after we place our order with the attentive waiter I say with curiosity, "Are you having a good time?"

"Lovely thanks, and you?"

"Great." We both look down and I know we are obviously accomplished liars because our words mean nothing and we both know it.

Changing direction, I say quickly, "Were you one of the competition winners?"

"Yes, were you?"

"No." I roll my eyes. "Charles is here on business."

"Nice business to be in." She laughs softly and I nod.

"It's ok, I guess, but to be honest, he hasn't done a lot of business since we arrived. The owner asked for one meeting and left him to it."

"The owner."

"I think he's called Mr Wheeler."

Kim looks interested, but we are interrupted when Charles heads our way and drops the bags on the seat beside me and takes the one next to Kim.

"You certainly know how to spend my money." He makes a joke of it, but I hear the steel edge to his voice and look at him in surprise. This isn't like Charles. He's always encouraged me to overspend, and I wonder why he's so edgy. Once again, the worry deepens and leaves me feeling unsettled and I feel regret burning a river of shame through me. Grabbing a glass of water, I gulp it down and say weakly, "Excuse me, I need to use the toilet."

Scraping back my chair, I avoid eye contact with either of them and head inside the cool interior of the café, glad of an excuse to get away even for a minute.

Once inside, I splash some water on my face and stare at the image of a woman who has sunk to her lowest point. How could I have done that, what was I thinking?

Part of me hates what I've done, and part of me applauds myself. One thing I know is, it can't happen again. It must be a one off, a delicious memory to get me through an emotionless life. Maybe I should use it as a catalyst to drive change because I can't go on the way I am. I need to make a break and put myself first because if it's taught me anything, it's that my marriage is over and I need to ask Charles for a divorce just as soon as we return home.

CHAPTER 21

EMMA

*B*en's boat is as impressive as the man. We take a short trip around the island and I am feeling hot for more reasons than the sun that is beating down and reflecting off the wake from the boat. Ben is attentive, kind and slightly intense, and I'm loving his company.

He points out various landmarks and offers a potted history of the island. After a while, I decide to delve a little deeper into his life and smile at him with interest.

"This must have cost a lot of money to develop. Is this your main business?"

He nods and leans on the rail, looking out to sea, and sounds almost pensive. "No, it's just another investment. I have several and as they say, money makes money, so if I'm careful, one investment funds the next and now I have a substantial portfolio."

It strikes me that Ben can't be much older than me, and I guess he had wealthy parents to set him on the right path. I lean on the rail next to him and say with a husky edge to my voice, "Your parents must be very proud."

"They are."

He gives nothing away and I shift a little closer. "Tell me about them."

He says nothing and just gazes broodingly at the ocean and then half turns and stares into my eyes. "I would rather learn about Emma Stone. What's her story?"

I smile and bat my eyelashes because I am fast discovering more than just a passing interest in the enigmatic man beside me. "There's not a lot to tell, really. I own a business making cakes." I laugh self-consciously.

"It's only just starting up and is quite challenging, to put it mildly."

"In what way?"

"In every way."

He looks interested and I shrug. "I can't afford help and just spend most of my time making the stock without any idea of where it's going. Then I run around trying to sell the product and end up giving most of it away just so they use me next time."

"Then you need to stop."

"What running around, or making cakes?"

"Everything."

His words irritate me and I say, feeling slightly offended. "Why?"

"Because you have no business plan. You have a product but no road to market. Take some time, research other companies in your field and work out best practice, other-wise you will fail, if you haven't already."

His words are brutal, but I know he means well, so I sigh and nod my head. "You're right, I know you are. I had thought this holiday would help me refocus." I laugh, "And I was right."

He turns and looks back across the ocean, and I feel a little desperate. I like him – a lot, and I want him to notice me as a woman, a potential love interest perhaps but he is reserved and not giving me any signs, so I say brightly, "Do you have a family, children maybe, or are you still searching?" I cringe at the desperation in my voice and he smiles. "Still looking." He turns and looks at me long and hard and it lights a heated trail through my body. "What about you?"

"Still looking." We share a smile, and then one of the stewards interrupts. "Mr Wheeler, we will dock in five minutes unless you wish to continue on somewhere else."

Praying for the latter, I'm disappointed when he says briskly, "No, we are done here."

He straightens up and stares at me, a faint smile ghosting his lips. "Have dinner with me, Emma, tonight, on my balcony."

"That sounds nice, thank you."

He nods and leans forward, his breath grazing my cheeks and whispers, "The pleasure will be all mine."

The boat shudders to a stop, making me fall against him and he reaches out to steady me and as soon as I feel his hands on me, it's like an electric charge bringing my body to life again. He is so close we could kiss but he just sets me straight and pulls away, saying evenly, "I will look forward to our evening, I'm afraid I have work to do but hope you enjoy your day. I have taken the liberty of booking you a full body massage and facial in the spa at 3pm. Complimentary, of course."

He smiles and I stare at him in surprise, swooning inside like a lovesick maiden. "Thank you."

I'm not sure what else to say and he offers me his arm. "Shall we?"

As I take it, I cling on tight because now I have met the man behind all this luxury, I have only one business plan in mind - make him mine and I have exactly six days to make that happen.

Ben leaves me and heads off to his office, or wherever it is he goes to work and I head to my room to change into my bikini and grab my kindle. I feel quite upbeat and hopeful for the future, and as soon as I step foot inside my room, I gasp at the sheer number of beautiful bouquets that welcome me in. It's like a florist shop in here, and as I dance around the room in delight, I feel my heart soaring as I inhale the intoxicating scent and admire their beauty. There is a handwritten card propped up against the largest one, and I seize it eagerly.

Beautiful flowers for a beautiful lady.
Until tonight, Ben xx

I actually hug myself and squeal with delight, feeling excited, exhilarated and as if I'm the luckiest girl alive. Things like this don't happen to me. It's like I've stepped into a romance novel in the starring role. Who needs a kindle when experience counts for so much more and I'm already planning my lingerie for later because I am going all the way on this? Opportunities like this don't come around often, and I am seizing this one and hanging on tight.

CHAPTER 22

*A*s soon as Evelyn leaves us, Charles turns his attention to me. "What happened?"

Swirling my finger around the rim of the glass, I say sadly, "Jack has ended it. Told me he wants us to separate. He doesn't even want to try, and there's not much I can do about that, is there?"

To my surprise, he reaches out and takes my hand, stroking it lightly and says kindly, "Then he's a fool."

"Thank you and yes, he is."

I smile at him but move my hand away because I am feeling a little uncomfortable with his attention. I know I'm attracted to him; I was the first time I saw him but he has a wife and a beautiful one at that. I'm not going to interfere with their happiness, so I smile and say firmly, "Anyway, you have been so kind and I really appreciate it but…"

"No, Kim."

"I'm sorry."

He smiles. "You were going to make your excuses and leave out of politeness. You feel as if you're intruding on our day, you're not. You think I am happy with my wife; I'm not.

The reason I want to help you is that I see my own situation in yours. Evelyn has withdrawn from our marriage and is not the woman I thought she was. Like your husband, she is desperately searching for a way out and she thinks I don't see that."

"I'm sorry." I stare at him with compassion and he shrugs. "It's not ideal, I'll give you that, but surely it's better to cut something loose that's dragging you under. Better to remove any restraints so you gain your freedom to move on to pastures new. What do you say about that, Kim, are you ready to cut the cord to freedom?"

"Not really."

He looks surprised and I say sadly, "I love my husband, Charles, regardless of how he treats me. It has always been Jack, and despite everything, I count loyalty as one of my strongest character traits. The fact he doesn't want me is killing me inside, but I'm not prepared to give up on him after one day. So, I'm sorry for your situation, I understand what you must be going through but I need to work out my own path through this and only when I feel there is no hope left, will I accept this is happening at all."

He nods, but I can see I touched a nerve.

"Promise me one thing then."

"What?"

"When you reach that point, you will call me."

He removes a card from his jacket pocket and hands it to me. Looking down, I see his details and he says softly, "Look me up when you need a friend. I'll always be that – your friend. More if you like."

He sighs. "I'm not one to ignore an opportunity when I see it. This trip has made me see where I'm heading with Evelyn, and then I met you. A woman that interests me more than I thought possible and yes, I admit the timing's off, but I can't ignore how I feel. When you left me last night, I felt happy and I haven't done that for a long time. We enjoyed an evening doing something so simple, yet it was made exciting because it was with you. I thought of you when I woke up and it gave me a warm feeling inside and when I saw my wife, I felt disappointed she wasn't you. Does that make me a monster, Kim, because I hope you feel the same?"

Now I feel super awkward and don't know what to say. Luckily, I am spared from answering when I hear a terse, "Kim."

Looking up, I see Jack standing behind me and he doesn't look pleased.

"Oh, um, Jack, this is Charles." I turn to Charles and say timidly, "This is Jack, my husband."

There's an atmosphere between them and it feels awkward. Jack is glaring at him and Charles looks mildly irritated but smiles briefly and extends his hand. "I'm pleased to meet you, Jack."

At the same moment Evelyn appears and looks a little shocked as she stares between us, and I suppose it's because the mood is tense as the men look at one another coolly.

Charles turns to Evelyn, "This is Jack, Kim's husband, you may remember him from the resort."

Evelyn looks a little unsettled and Charles just stares at her with a strange expression in his eyes as she nods. "Yes, I'm pleased to meet you."

Charles waves to the seat with all the shopping bags and says to Jack, "Please join us for lunch."

Praying he refuses, I look at him with what I hope is a firm message in my eyes but Jack either doesn't see, or ignores it and says, "Thank you, I could use a drink."

Charles barks, "Evelyn, move your bags."

She jumps as if she's been shot and quickly moves the bags and Jack sits down and drapes his arm around my shoulders, pulling my chair away from Charles and making it obvious he's not happy finding me here at all. If anything, the gesture gives me hope and I stare at him in surprise as he orders a beer from the waiter who hovers hopefully nearby.

Charles looks at Jack with a superior look and says loudly, "So, are you enjoying your stay, I understand you won it on Facebook?"

"Kim did. I never bother with social media."

Charles nods. "Then we agree on something. Evelyn is on it more than she should be; it can't be good for you."

He looks between us and says brightly, "Maybe you should send each other a friend request, isn't that what people do when they meet a fellow user?"

Evelyn smiles politely, "Of course, I'll look you up."

As I stare at her, I feel a surge of pity for the woman I envied not that long ago. Seeing her with Charles is a strange experience because it's as if something is seriously off about their relationship. She seems nervous around him and on edge, and it feels awkward and strange being in their company. Jack is also brooding about something and I expect it's the state of our marriage and I wish I was anywhere other than here.

The conversation is stilted and unnatural and after a while Jack says shortly, "Well, thanks for your company but we should leave, the boat will be waiting and there's somewhere I want to show Kim first."

I look at him in surprise but don't hesitate in jumping up because the sooner I'm away from this strange couple, the better.

Charles smiles politely and Evelyn just looks relieved and as we walk away, Jack takes my hand and grips it hard.

It's not until we turn the corner that he drops it and says angrily, "What the hell are you playing at, Kim?"

"What do you mean?"

"I saw you holding that man's hand; what's this, lining up your next victim before the last one's even cold?"

He looks so angry it throws me a little before I recover and hiss, "For your information, Charles was just being kind. He found me last night after you left me on the beach and saved me."

"Saved you from what?"

Jack laughs bitterly and I snarl. "I thought someone was in the bushes and felt afraid. Charles was the first person I ran into, and he made sure I was safe. He checked the bushes, then arranged a drink at the bar to steady my nerves. He was kind and considerate, which I really needed when I discovered my husband wanted to call time on our marriage."

"So you were with him until the early hours, that's some drink you had, or was it something else he gave you?"

Jack looks so annoyed it shocks me a little and I reply angrily, "How dare you judge me after your behaviour. Charles was there for me when my husband wasn't. It was the same again today. You left me in a strange town on my own because you just can't deal with your decision. Well, for your information, I don't need this and I'm increasingly realising I don't need you. So back off and leave me alone because you are seriously deluded if you think any part of your behaviour is acceptable."

I turn away and Jack sighs. "I'm sorry, Kim."

His apologetic tone stops me in my tracks and he says sadly, "My mind's all over the place, and I'm sorry. Listen, let's draw a line under this and head back. I'm not sure I want to end this after all."

I stare at him in surprise and he smiles ruefully. "I suppose I'm at a crossroads and don't know where to turn. Maybe I'm having a mid-life crisis, who knows, but seeing you with him, another man, it taught me something."

"What?"

He steps closer and takes my hands, staring deeply into my eyes. "I don't want to give up on us just yet."

He leans in and presses his lips to mine and pulls me hard against him, and I think I fall into a state of shock. What's happening, my emotions are all over the place right now and I don't know how I feel, or what I want anymore?

CHAPTER 23

CHLOE

I hold John's hand tightly as we board the boat, desperately trying not to make eye contact with anyone in case it's him. I know I should tell John; he has a right to know, but I can't. The man would probably deny it, say he was just passing the time of day and I can't revisit how I felt after I was attacked all those years ago. Nobody believed me at first. They thought I was drunk and covering my stupidity. It's only when they found the traces of Rohypnol in my system that it became an investigation. The man was never caught, and I have had to live with the consequences of that ever since.

It hurts just thinking about the repercussions, which is why I remain silent now. It's just not worth the drama it would bring.

John squeezes my hand tightly, "Is everything ok, love? You've gone quiet on me."

"It's fine." I flash him a bright smile, probably a little too bright because I see the questions in his eyes.

"I think I'm still a little jet-lagged, if I'm honest."

He nods. "Yes, it's been a full-on day, straight after

another one. Maybe we can relax by the pool for a few hours' rest before dinner."

I nod but feel my skin crawl as I picture that man opposite me ogling my body as I soak up the sun. Just the fact he was there yesterday tells me he will be again, and it has now ruined what was a dream holiday.

I notice the other couples nearby and see the many bags the rich looking woman's husband is carrying. John leans down and whispers, "The perks of having a first-class luggage allowance, she's obviously shopped till she dropped, she looks as if she's about to keel over."

I glance at the woman and admit he's right. She looks worse than I feel and I wonder if she's ok. Her husband appears a little angry too, and it's obvious they've had an argument, just by the fact they can't look at one another.

The other couple seem happier than when we arrived, and he sits with his arm draped around her shoulders as he strokes her hair lovingly. She doesn't seem that pleased about it though, and it looks as if he has some making up to do.

The fact a shiver passes through me, tells me the man is somewhere close. It's as if I have a sixth sense, and I stare down at my hands rather than make eye contact with a monster. As the engine starts, I say quickly, "Shall we head to the front of the boat, we could watch out for dolphins or something."

John nods. "Sounds good to me, we have to make the most of all our opportunities because they don't come around that often, after all."

We make our way to the front and it feels good to be away from the crowd. The fresh air and spray from the ocean cleanse my spirit and as I snuggle up beside my man, it's difficult to think back to a time when my life was so dark. I was at rock bottom, the lowest a person can go and somehow, over time and perseverance, I stepped away from it all. I pushed the bad memories away and left them behind me, at least I thought I had. In one sentence that man has brought them all crashing back and once again, I wonder if I should confide in John.

I suppose the reason I haven't is that I have done my best to forget such a traumatic memory. It didn't end at the hospital either. I endured interviews with the police, social workers, counsellors, and I suppose what happened after was even more devastating than the event itself.

At least I wasn't conscious during the attack, but I endured a living nightmare for years after. Just thinking of either of my daughters going through what I did, makes me super protective of them, which is why I keep them with me as much as possible.

Until now.

Now I have anxiety just thinking of Sasha going out with her friends. The fact she has a boyfriend is also making me feel sick inside. If anything ever happened to either one of them, it would destroy me, and I suppose that's what makes my mind up for me. I must tell John. He needs to understand the reasons for my often strange behaviour and so I vow to tell him on this holiday and what better opener than what happened today.

"Excuse me."

A woman's voice interrupts my thoughts and we both turn around and see the lady with the shopping looking apologetic. "You dropped these."

She smiles and hands me my sunglasses, and I laugh self-consciously. "Thank you."

She turns to leave and I say quickly, "Are you enjoying your stay?"

"Yes, it's lovely, are you?"

"It's beautiful, we are very lucky."

She nods and heads back and John shakes his head. "She's a strange one."

"I thought she was nice."

"You would. No, I see it in the way she holds herself. She's unhappy, it's obvious, and no prizes for guessing why."

"Why?"

He rolls his eyes. "This isn't like you, Chloe, you normally spot the gossip way before me."

"What gossip?"

He lowers his voice, "The two couples over there can't look one another in the face. The woman who brought you the glasses is pointedly ignoring her husband and keeps on stealing looks at the other woman's husband. He, meanwhile, is staring angrily at the other man and his wife is angry with him. What do you think happened, a swinging session that ended badly, perhaps?"

Despite myself, I laugh. "You've got a dirty mind, John."

He runs his arm around my waist and squeezes me tightly. "Do you want to see how dirty it is? I'll show you if you like as soon as we get back."

Giggling, I smile up at him. "If you like."

He laughs and dips his head to kiss me softly and suddenly that one small act makes everything alright again with my world. As long as I have John beside me, I have everything.

CHAPTER 24

EMMA

I keep on pinching myself because things like this don't happen to me. Ben arranged the most amazing pamper session for me this afternoon, and I have never felt so relaxed. The massage made me feel better than I have done in years, and my skin is positively glowing after the facial. The spa itself is state-of-the-art, and it certainly gave me an insight into a world I would love to make mine.

For the entire afternoon, I have dreamed of what it would be like to be part of this world. Part of Ben's life and it's not just the money that attracts, it's the man himself. There's something intense, dark and mysterious that sparks my interest and the more time I spend in his company, the more I don't want to leave.

I tried to engage the beautician in conversation, to discover more about my enigmatic host, but she knew nothing about him. I'm not surprised though because it's all new here and the staff have only just arrived.

So, as I make my way to my room, I look forward to doing some research of my own while I'm here, using my iPad because there must be some information on him some-where online.

When I reach my room, the scent hits me before the vision of the beautiful flowers that take up most of the space on every surface. I feel so happy I could skip around the room and coupled with how amazing I feel, I never want to wake up from this glorious dream.

Pushing open the doors to the balcony, I venture outside and breathe in the unpolluted air of an island paradise and sink onto the sun-bed for some much-needed sunbathing.

I must have only been back for five minutes before there's a knock on the door and I groan and grab my towel and head inside to open it.

I'm surprised to see the housekeeper smiling pleasantly at me outside.

"Miss Stone, I'm sorry for the interruption, I hope you are enjoying your day."

"Yes, thank you, I can't fault a thing."

She nods and to my surprise, hands me a large white box tied with a pink satin bow.

"Special delivery."

She smiles. "For you, compliments of Mr Wheeler. He has also instructed me to tell you that he will call for you at 7 pm."

I feel myself blushing as I take the box and she steps back. "Good afternoon, Miss Stone."

As she turns away, I say quickly, "Excuse me, Mrs Chloris…"

"Yes, madam."

"Well, I just wondered how well you know Mr Wheeler?" She looks surprised and I squirm a little.

"I don't, Miss Stone. He is my employer, and I have little to do with him. We are all new here and still finding our way."

"Of course, it's just that… well. I've never had this much attention before, and I was curious about the man behind it."

"Then enjoy it, Miss Stone, I know I would." She winks before turning away, and there is a warm glow inside me as I close the door behind her.

Eagerly, I head into the bedroom and sit on the oversized bed and untie the ribbon to reveal the secret inside the box. My fingers shake a little as I part the scented tissue and reveal a beautiful red evening gown nestling inside. I stare in shock as I pull it out and feel the soft, luxurious, silky fabric slip through my fingers and stare in amazement at a creation that must have cost a small fortune. I can tell quality when I see it, and this is way more than my meagre budget would allow. Then I notice a small white box nestling underneath the tissue paper and my fingers shake as I pull it free and open it, revealing a stunning diamond choker.

My mouth drops open as I hold the diamonds in my hand, and I shake a little as I buckle under the weight of desire. Desire for the lifestyle, the gifts and the man himself. This is heady stuff and almost unbelievable. The holiday itself was the stuff of magic but this, this is text book fairy tale.

ON THE DOT OF SEVEN, there's a sharp knock on the door and I shiver inside. This is it, he's here. I take one last look at my reflection in the mirror and see a woman balancing on the edge of happily ever after. My hair is freshly washed and styled in loose curls and my make-up is subtle, yet designed to accentuate my best features. Red lipstick stains my lips and complements the amazing red dress that fits like a glove. The diamonds sparkle at my throat and I have never looked or felt as good as I do now.

Nervously, I head to the door and my mouth drops open when I see him standing there, watching me with that intense look that dives straight into my soul.

"You look beautiful, Emma."

His deep voice makes me shiver inside and wraps me in desire. He is dressed immaculately in black trousers with a white formal shirt, slightly open, revealing a tanned broad chest. His dark hair is freshly washed and slightly damp from the shower and his dark eyes glitter with what I'm hoping is desire. His beard is trimmed and his glasses look stylish on him, and I can see they are an expensive brand by the logo on the side.

As his hand reaches for mine, I note the expensive watch on his wrist and he pulls me slightly closer and drops his mouth to my ear, his lips brushing against my skin and his breath hot on my face.

"Are you hungry, Emma?"

I nod and edge slightly closer because the hunger I have is not for the food and he smiles. "Then I hope you will like what I have planned."

We start walking down the hallway towards the lift and I say in a slightly breathy voice, "Thank you for the dress, the necklace, the massage and well, just thank you for everything."

"It was my pleasure."

He grips my hand a little tighter and when we reach the lift, he looks at me and smiles. "I didn't like the idea of you dining alone. I know how lonely that can be, so I thought we could double up, make a night of it and enjoy some company for a change."

We step inside the lift and I hesitate, before saying, "I'm surprised you're on your own. I would have thought you'd find it easy to meet someone."

He shakes his head. "No, I have no one, I never had the

time to meet anyone because all of this takes up most of it."

"What, you've never been married, or met the right woman, I can relate to that, it's not as easy as you think it is?"

"I agree, but what about you, Emma, why are you still single, if you are that is?"

"I have just never found the right man. Nobody ever measured up, really. There was always something about them that I didn't like, and I suppose I'm striving for perfection where it concerns my heart."

"I completely understand."

I smile. "Do you?"

He nods. "I strive for perfection in every aspect of my life and never settle for anything less. This resort is the culmination of a lifelong dream. A perfect escape. The reason you work so hard all year just for a few days of paradise to make it all worthwhile. It would have been so easy to build a resort that catered to the masses. Fill the rooms with average furnishings and open up the doors to a less discerning clientele. But I want the best, Emma. I want perfection and I know there are people out there who share my desires. The fact we are booked solidly for the next year tells me I was right. So, now my dream is realised, I am turning my attention to the next part of my plan."

"Which is?"

The doors open and he takes my hand again, before lifting it to his lips and pressing them lightly down on my skin, before saying, "I am looking for love, Emma, the final part of my life plan that will deliver me a family. A woman of rare beauty and intellect who will share my life and passions."

My heart is beating furiously as his eyes convey his meaning far more than his words and it appears that I am the front runner in this and I'm now determined to be the first past the winning post.

CHAPTER 25

*C*harles is brooding on something and I am wrapped in so many emotions I'm finding it difficult to concentrate. Seeing Jack with his wife compounded my misery, and I hated every minute of it. Charles also seems to have developed a weird fascination for her, unless he is using her to bring me back in line by showing me there is always a replacement for my position and that I need to step up and protect my investment. I know how his mind works and he has obviously noticed the cooling off of our relationship.

I don't think we spoke two words on the journey back to the room and as we step inside, he surprises me by saying lightly, "Kim seems nice."

"Yes, she does."

"Her husband is a little intense though."

"Really, I hadn't noticed."

He surprises me by laughing loudly. "If you say so, darling. You see, you forget I'm a man who prides himself on knowing everything about the people closest to him. I saw the way you reacted when he arrived, it made you uncomfortable and that interested me. I saw you darting little looks in his direction and the fact that he ignored you for most of the time, told me everything I wanted to know. You like him. You are attracted to the man and that, my darling wife, was all I needed to make up my mind."

"What are you talking about, I don't even know him?"

"Maybe not, but you would like to."

He turns and the look he gives me makes my blood run cold. "You've changed, Evelyn. The past few months, possibly even a year, I've watched you become more disillusioned with life. You no longer find excitement in the material things I give you. You tolerate my company and have become cold and unfeeling, which leads me to wonder why?"

I stare at him in shock because he never seems to pay much attention to me outside the obvious and I shake my head. "You really don't know?"

"No, I don't."

Taking a deep breath, I try to control my words because Charles is a business man who would appreciate emotion being kept out of this discussion. Maybe he needs to hear this and perhaps he will actually listen, so I say sadly, "The thing is, Charles, you give me everything I could possibly need or want and it's a little stifling at times. You have moulded me into a version of your perfect woman and it's crushing my spirit."

His eyes flash, but he nods. "Go on."

Sighing, I sit on the edge of the bed and fix him with a sad look. "I keep on trying to tell you that I want more. Not materially speaking but I want something to engage my brain. A job, something to rekindle my interest for life. A routine, something to call my own and a reason to get up in the morning. I know you will find this hard to believe, but I need to work. To feel as if I'm contributing in some way to our life. Something to talk about over dinner as we compare notes on our day because currently I have zero conversation.

This isn't me, Charles, I'm not a barbie doll that you can dress and style their hair. I am better than that and yet you won't allow me my freedom and it's destroying me."

To my surprise, he sits beside me on the bed and takes my hand, and I think that alone nearly causes my heart to fail.

His voice is almost sad, wistful even, as he strokes his thumb across my hand. "I'm sorry, Evelyn, you're right, I never listened. I thought you loved the life I have created for us, most women would, and I suppose I was so blinded by my need to make our world perfect, I never considered what you wanted."

I think I'm in shock as my husband actually opens up a little to me and he turns to face me and smiles. "I know what would make everything better."

"Really," I face him with a renewed hope that this relationship isn't as dead as I think it is because the man looking at me so lovingly is the man I fell in love with all those years ago.

"Evelyn, I worshipped you from the day you walked into my office as that new assistant I badly needed. You were so beautiful and faced me with a bravery that made me smile. It was your first proper job, and I knew you had taken care to present yourself in a way you thought was required. The smart suit, the ponytail and perfect make up. I saw behind that, I saw the yearning for more, for making things work and doing your best. Over the next few months, you never let me down once. Everything I asked, you carried out efficiently and without comment. I know I worked you hard, pushed you to your limits, but you never complained. I fell in love with you every hour and every minute since the day I met you, and all I wanted was to make you smile."

I am mesmerised by the sadness in his voice and seduced by the memories. It takes me back to a time when I would have done anything for this man. We worked as a team, and I loved every minute of it. Maybe that's why I'm struggling, because I was the happiest I have ever been when I worked alongside him. The past few years have proved that to me because now I feel empty, have no purpose and no desire for the life he has provided. I'm almost afraid to ask and yet I have to now I've started the conversation that is long over-due, so I say nervously, "I want that back, Charles, I want what we had back then."

He nods and I see a shadow cross his face as he sighs. "I loved you, Evelyn, a little too much possibly. I never wanted a family; I never wanted to see my baby grow inside you, changing your body and causing you discomfort. I always wanted you to remain perfect, to be the woman I fell in love with, and I never wanted to share you. I understand now that was selfish of me and it's no wonder you're struggling because it's in every woman's DNA to want children. I know what this is, what's missing from our lives, and the sense of fulfilment, of purpose, can only be attributed to one thing, a baby."

I stare at him in shock as he moves his hand and pats my flat stomach and says huskily, "You don't need a job, darling, you need a baby and I am being cruel in denying you that."

He smiles. "Stop taking the pills, Evelyn, I will allow you one child as my gift to you. Something to occupy your time and give your life meaning. A project of the most loving kind, and I will also entrust the remodelling of our new home to your capable hands. Yes, you need a project and what better one than that. It's what women want after all, and I am man enough to admit my mistakes and accept I was wrong."

Words fail me as he stands and looks pleased with himself, as if he has just closed a business deal to his satisfac-tion. I open my mouth to speak, but no words come out as he says more confidently, "We will order room service this evening. If you like, you may go to the gym or have a swim and relax by the pool because I have work to do. You know, I'm glad we had this chat, I feel as if it has chased away a few storm clouds and now the sky is bright again.

He leaves me sitting on the bed, staring after him in disbelief. How does he get it so wrong every time? The last thing I want is a child – with him. That would add another link to the chain binding me to his side and the only thing I want more than air right now, is my freedom - from him.

CHAPTER 26

KIM

I think I'm living in a parallel universe. Jack appears to have gone full circle and is back to the fun-loving husband I love the most. I am seriously worried about his mental health because he is trying so hard to make things up to me. Maybe it was seeing Charles's interest that fed the beast inside him. He's always had a possessive streak and was obviously unhappy about seeing me with another man.

I'm not interested in any other man, I never was and yet, I saw the interest Charles had for me and to be honest, it was a little intense and quite scary really. When I saw him at the airport, I would have given anything for a man like that. The trouble is, it wasn't him I wanted, I wanted my husband to be *like* him, not him physically. When I looked at the family and the way the couple took pleasure in each other and their children, I wanted that – with Jack. It's always been Jack, which is why it's been so hard knowing he doesn't appear to want the same things.

We have avoided the conversation we should have had the moment we reached our room but Jack was keen to get to the pool and enjoy the facilities and I'm much the same.

We spent the afternoon relaxing and making polite conversation and for now I am happy about that. We need to enjoy this break, not rock the boat and try to find a way forward out of the corner we appear to have backed ourselves into.

In fact, we are both so intent on avoiding the conversation we know is imminent, we just paper over the cracks and carry on as usual.

Dinner is a quiet affair and as we reach the restaurant, it feels as if several people are missing. I am surprised by the number of empty tables and wonder why they invited such a select gathering to test the facilities.

Jack is drinking rather a lot and I worry about that as well. I know he's unhappy, there's something seriously wrong with our relationship and I suppose if I'm honest, there has been for some time.

After an awkward meal, Jack sighs heavily. "What do you want to do?"

"I'm not sure, do you have any ideas?"

"Not really, I'm quite tired though, maybe we should just call it a night and hope tomorrow is a better day."

"Yes, I think you're right."

He nods and makes to leave and I sigh inside, remembering the time he would insist on holding my hand, making sure I was happy before anything else. Now it's as if we are strangers and I'm not sure how we can go forward from this.

Luckily, there is no sign of Charles or Evelyn, which I'm glad about because they set me on edge. I'm not sure why but Evelyn seems so wrapped in shadows it makes me feel uncomfortable. I didn't miss the surreptitious glances she threw Jack's way and the fact he studiously ignored her just isn't like him. He seemed keen enough to look at her on the ride from the airport and knowing my husband, I'm guessing there has been some kind of contact between them.

We head back to our room and as Jack pushes open the

door, I am surprised to see an envelope pushed under it. Jack bends down and retrieves it and tears it open, revealing an invitation inside and he reads it out sounding a little annoyed.

Ladies, you are cordially invited to a spa gathering at 9am tomorrow, followed by lunch on the terrace.
Gentlemen, you are invited to spend the morning on the resort boat The Lotus, where you can enjoy snorkelling, swimming and relaxation massages with our resident masseuse.
Compliments of the management of The Lotus Lake Resort and Spa.

Jack groans. "Great, just what I need, to be confined on a boat with strangers. Well, I won't be going."

"Well, I will. Honestly, Jack, this is an opportunity of a lifetime and we should enjoy everything the resort has to offer. It's up to you if you want to miss out just because you're in a bad mood."

"I think it's more than just a bad mood, wouldn't you say."

"I'm not sure what it is but one thing's certain, we can't go on like this. Your moods are all over the place and I don't know what to think anymore. I can't cope with it and if you don't sort your head out, I'm not sure this marriage can continue. Personally, I think a day apart is just what we need to work out what we both really want out of this marriage."

To my surprise, Jack sighs and sits down heavily on the bed and puts his head in his hands. "I'm sorry, Kim."

A bad feeling creeps around my heart like an unwanted virus.

"For what?" My voice sounds calm but inside my heart is racing and as he raises his eyes to mine, he looks shattered.

"I can't pretend anymore, I've kept something back from you and I can't live with it, you deserve better."

"Ok."

I'm not sure I want to hear what he's about to say but he obviously needs to get it off his chest, so I sit beside him awkwardly and say slightly nervously, "What is it?"

He takes a deep breath and says roughly, "I can't give you what you want, I can't be the husband you deserve and it's tearing me up inside."

"In what way?"

He reaches over and takes my hand. "I can't have children."

The tears sting as he voices something I have suspected for some time.

"I can't be the husband you need, Kim. I know how much you want children but I can't give you the one thing you want above everything. Don't you think I see the way you look at them, the yearning in your eyes, the small smile on your face as you imagine your own. It pains me to watch and know that can never be us. I've let you down and I wouldn't blame you if you wanted to call time on our marriage."

"I don't."

If I'm sure of anything, it's that because despite the way he acts sometimes, I do love my husband, very much as it happens.

"Do you know why, I mean, there could be a way around it? Perhaps there's another way, IVF, egg fertilisation, we can't give up."

"Just stop, Kim."

I recoil at the harsh anger in his voice as he hisses. "Do you think I'd be telling you this if I thought there was a chance, there isn't."

"But..."

"Enough, I don't want to talk about it. I don't want to discuss other ways, adoption, surrogacy, or any crazy scheme you may concoct. I just want a childless future with, or without you by my side."

I stare at him in shock as he stands and heads towards the bathroom. "Now, that's finally in the open, I'll leave you to decide what you want to do about it. If you love me and not what I can give you, then this marriage may just work. If you were just looking for a sperm donor, I'm sure there will be someone only too happy to oblige but I'm gone."

He slams the bathroom door, leaving me reeling. For a moment I'm too shocked to react and then that stupid voice in my head that always excuses everything he does, starts telling me to be compassionate. He's obviously destroyed by this and is using anger to vent his frustrations. He will calm down and we can discuss this rationally and I must be empathetic, considerate and understanding. I'm his wife and my vows counted for something and we will work through this problem together because above everything, I want him.

But do I?

The other voice in my head starts up and whispers, 'But what about you and what you want? Is he really the love of your life? Think about the lonely nights you spend waiting for him to come home without telling you where he's been. What about the violent rages he flies into at the least little thing? Is it right that he belittles you and makes you feel as if you are lucky to have him, and what about the wandering eye and obvious affairs he has? Is Jack really the man for you, or the man that's just beside you at this moment in time, or was he just a big mistake, delivered to you in a haze of lust and broken promises? You deserve better than this and you always have.'

I wander out onto the balcony and the cool breeze acts as a balm, soothing the sting in my eyes. A huge wave of sadness washes over me as I think about the life I have made for myself. At the centre of everything is my husband. The devastating man who I fell so deeply in love with, I forgive him every indiscretion, every harsh word and every horrible thing he has ever said to me. The fact he won't even discuss this is him all over. He keeps himself unreadable, a locked book with a key that only he can find. Do I really know my husband? I already know I don't.

Maybe he's right, I should find someone else but I can't appear to see beyond him. He obscures my view from what else is out there and maybe I should edge past him and see what's there but I already know I'm not strong enough for that because despite everything, I love my husband and nothing can cure a person of that.

CHAPTER 27

CHLOE

*I*t feels a little strange without John beside me. When we got the invitation, I was secretly glad about it. Not because I don't want to spend time with John, but because I want to be in a safe place where no men are allowed because then I won't have to see *him*. The man who was in my dreams last night, merging with my attacker. Suddenly, my attacker had a face, and I woke up sweating and shaking as he invaded my subconscious.

John can tell something is up, but I reassured him I was just worried about the girls, which made him angry as it usually does. He doesn't understand my need to keep them safe. I know I'm over protective but I'm allowed to be - surely.

He complained about spending time with strangers and was quite irritable this morning at breakfast, grumbling that this wasn't what he had in mind when we stepped on board that plane.

However, I can't think about it now because that invitation was a welcome intervention and may just enable me to get my head straight so we can carry on with this holiday of a lifetime without worry.

"Hi."

The pretty woman who I saw at the pool on the first day approaches and I smile. "Hi."

She stops and whispers, "I'm not going to lie, I'm in paradise right now, this place is seriously amazing."

"It certainly is."

I stare at her with envy when I see her slim figure in a tight-fitting sundress and long shapely legs tapering to a tiny waist. Thinking of my own figure makes me suck it in a little as I look at the women surrounding me. The glamorous woman I saw with her husband on the trip is looking bored already and yet she still radiates beauty and a fashion sense that looks thrown together but must have cost a small fortune. The woman opposite her looks lost in thought and I admire her sharp blonde bob and envious figure. In fact, I feel like a fish out of water among these glamorous women and feel glad of the loose-fitting top that covers my swollen stomach, after two children stretched it and left it resembling a deflated balloon.

"Anyway, I'm Emma." She holds out her hand and I smile. "Chloe." We shake hands and she lowers her voice.

"You know, I won this holiday on Facebook, that's crazy, isn't it?"

"Me too." I laugh softly and she shakes her head.

"Do you think the other women did as well?"

"Probably."

She looks at me with interest. "Are you here with your husband, I saw you with a man by the pool?"

"Well, sort of."

I laugh as she raises her eyes. "He is in every sense of the word, just not on paper."

"So, you never actually married, I suppose that's normal these days."

"Yes, I suppose it is."

She sighs and says wistfully, "I'd love to be married. Plan a wedding, invite all my family and friends, you know, the big party and all that comes with it. In fact, I have a whole Pinterest board devoted to my wedding when I finally get someone to ask."

"That sounds – exhausting." I laugh and she grins.

"It is, but worth it. So, what about you, did you ever want to get married?"

"Yes, I always wanted it but life kind of overtook us and we had the house and family before the wedding and now money is so tight, we can't afford it."

She stares at me with sympathy. "You could always do it abroad, here perhaps. Maybe that would be the cheaper option, just the two of you with strangers as witnesses. I've heard it's all the rage these days."

"Possibly."

Luckily, we are interrupted when a pretty woman heads our way and smiles. "Welcome ladies, I'm Bianca and I'm your hostess for today. Firstly, I'd like to welcome you to the Lotus spa and tell you a little about what you can expect. First you can change into your bikinis and robes and then relax with a welcome fruit smoothie, guaranteed to restore energy and vitality. We use only the freshest ingredients and pride ourselves on offering perfection. Then you can use the pool, steam rooms, saunas and hot tub. Each of you has a program of treatments lined up, which include mud therapy, massage and beauty." She laughs "By the end of this session you will feel like a new woman before enjoying a healthy lunch and after you can relax by the pool, or in your rooms. Any questions please come and find me and I will only be too happy to help. So, if you follow me, we can get started."

It doesn't take long before we are changed and relaxing by a huge indoor swimming pool. I sit beside Emma, who looks amazing in a green bikini as she sips on a fruit cocktail before lowering her voice. "You know, this holiday is shaping up to be the best I've ever had."

"Yes, me too."

She looks excited and whispers, "You know, Chloe, I think I may just burst unless I tell someone what happened to me yesterday."

I feel a prickle of tension grab me as I remember what happened to me yesterday, and yet from the look in her eyes, her experience was a happy one.

"I met someone."

"Who?"

"Well…" her eyes get that dreamy faraway look that only the besotted have, and she smiles. "It's like a fairy tale. I have been inundated since I arrived with flowers, cocktails, chocolates, amazing service and quite honestly thought it was part of the deal."

"Who sent them then?" From the look on her face, whoever it was meets her approval because she sighs. "The owner of this resort, Ben."

"Really?" I sense a bunch of red flags waving because I'm already cynical as I see this for what it could be. A beautiful young woman all alone in unfamiliar territory. The perfect prey for a man with only one thing on his mind. Suddenly, a horrible feeling grabs me and I hope to god it's not that sleazy man by the pool. What if he's the owner and is targeting Emma now?

She says dreamily, "Last night was the best night of my life."

A feeling of unease grips me as she says softly, "He arranged dinner for us on a private terrace overlooking the ocean. He had a beautiful silk dress delivered to my room with a diamond choker, and then he called for me. You know, Chloe, I never thought dreams could come true and I've waited long enough for mine but Ben, well, he is everything I imagined in those dreams of mine. Good looking, amazing company and rich, did I mention the rich part because this man is seriously loaded."

"What happened?" I almost daren't ask, and she shivers a little. "We had so much in common. The food was amazing, better than I've ever had, and the atmosphere was so romantic. We spoke about our dreams, wishes for the future and he told me his and you know what..."

"What?"

"They were the same as mine. Can you believe it, Chloe, my ship really came in when I won that competition because men like Ben aren't found in clubs and walking down the aisle of the supermarket?"

"So, what happened last night?"

She giggles and blushes a little. "Well, as I said, it was so romantic and I kind of fell under his spell a little. After dinner we went for a walk along the beach and he held my hand and asked me about myself. He was so interested in everything and all I wanted was for him to stop talking and kiss me."

"And did he, kiss you, I mean?"

I am riveted by her story and the romantic in me is swooning right now as she nods. "He did. It was the most romantic kiss of my life and he kissed me deeply and as if I was the most desirable woman in the world. He made me feel like a princess, and who can fight against that?"

"So, what happened next?"

She grins. "We kissed some more and then he took me back to the terrace where he had arranged a nightcap. There was a fire burning in a pit I hadn't noticed before, and a cashmere blanket that he wrapped around my shoulders. You know, Chloe, he was the perfect gentleman and I think I fell in love with him last night. Is that possible, do you think? Love at first date because I feel as if it is, possible that is."

Her excitement is infectious and I smile. "Yes, I think it is."

"Anyway, he was the perfect gentleman and at the end of the evening he escorted me to my room. I was so ready to invite him in because I'm conscious we don't have long, but he didn't give me the chance because he just kissed me softly on the hand and asked me if I would meet him tonight for dinner. He would like to show me a little place he goes to eat really good food with an amazing view. I really am living the dream, aren't I?"

"Yes, you are." I can't help but worrying about this woman though because it doesn't sound right to me and so I say hastily, "Are you sure it's a good idea to go somewhere other than the resort though? I mean, you still don't really know him."

"I know enough, Chloe. I googled him and his business is well documented online. He's quite a catch and is considered one of the most eligible bachelors in society, given the fact he's worth several millions. So, you can see why I'm so excited. This man is a gift from God and I am not returning it to sender."

Bianca appears and says reverently, "Emma, your masseuse is waiting and Chloe, the mud room has been prepared for you."

Emma jumps up with excitement. "Great, I'm looking forward to this if yesterday's is anything to go by."

"Yesterdays?"

She grins. "Another complimentary gift from Ben. Can that man get any better?"

CHAPTER 28

EVELYN

That invitation was a godsend because I couldn't stand another minute with Charles if I tried. He thinks he's solved all our problems by a throwaway comment, acting as if he has given me the biggest gift of all – a baby. Well, not if I have anything to do with it because the thought of having a child with him makes me feel physically sick.

Now I appear to be in hell because I have been partnered up with Kim, the woman who appears to have men falling at her feet, mine included.

I hate the fact I like her, really like her, because she has been so sweet to me since we were partnered up this morning.

"I could get used to this life."

Kim stretches out with contentment in the sauna and I nod. "It's certainly impressive."

She looks thoughtful. "This must be your life; please tell me it is because I'll be sorely disappointed if it's not."

She grins as I stare at her in surprise. "Why do you say that?"

She blushes a little and looks uncomfortable. "I'm sorry, it's just that I saw you in the airport and noted your luggage and the fact you were in first class. It made me smile seeing how attentive your husband was to you and I was a little jealous if I'm honest."

"Why, you were seated not far from us if I remember correctly?"

"Only because the stewardess took pity on me and moved me from travel hell."

I smile as she proceeds to tell me what happened, and I find myself liking her way more than I should. I'm even happy that her husband doesn't know, and I wonder how many secrets they keep from each other because I can think of two of them now.

Sighing, I study my immaculate fingernails and say sadly, "Looks can be deceptive. When I saw you at the airport, I was jealous of you."

"Me! Why on earth would you be jealous of me?"

"You seemed happy and your husband looked like a fun companion. Charles is a little stuffy most of the time and although I can't fault his generosity, or his manners, life with him is kind of dull."

"I'm sorry." She seems genuine and maybe it's because she's so kind and a stranger, I offload some of my problems.

"The sad thing is, Kim, my marriage is probably hanging on by a designer thread. Charles works all the time, all hours of the day and well into the night. Most of my time is spent on my own because I don't have many friends. They all have families, children and endless social engagements. I have shopping and the hairdressers with the occasional fitness class thrown in. Yes, I have a nice car, a nice house and an endless credit account, but that's not what I want."

"What do you want?"

"To work."

Her eyes widen and I laugh. "Yes, a little strange when most people dream of retirement, but I have always wanted to work. To have that buzz knowing you are achieving something. A place to go every day where you count for something. Friends and colleagues who become more like your family than your own and a sense of living your best life because when you don't have that, it's meaningless."

"Then why don't you get a job?"

"Charles won't listen when I tell him. He thinks what's missing is a baby to occupy my time. To be honest, I'm surprised he didn't buy me a puppy and have done with it. He thinks he just needs to tick a box and I'll be happy, while he heads back to business where he lives most days. In our marriage there are three things. Him, me and business. It sits between us like a third wheel because he would much rather spend time with that than me.

"Then tell him - go and get a job and he will have to accept it."

"Maybe, then again, you don't know Charles. He would hate it and make my life miserable until I gave it up. Anyway, what about you, do you work?"

Kim nods but has a sad look in her eye. "I'm a hairdresser. I work for a lovely woman called Betty, who, as you said, has become like a mother to me. I love working there, but Jack thinks I should set up on my own. Be more ambitious, when all I want is a family."

She laughs and shakes her head. "I think we need to swap places. It appears you got my dream, and I got yours."

We share a smile and I feel bad for what I've done with her husband. I know there is also a connection she shares with Charles, and I'm keen to learn what that is.

"I'm sorry, Kim, but..." I stop and she nods, "Go on."

"Well," I sigh heavily, "Did something happen with

Charles, it's just that you appeared familiar when we met in the town?"

She blushes a little and looks guilty. Maybe I should be angry, worried even, but there's a part of me that hopes she's about to tell me something that takes him off my hands, which shows how far my marriage has already deteriorated.

"The other night, Jack and I had an argument. He left me and rather than face the rest of you having a happy time, I headed back through the trees. For a while it felt as if someone was following me and I was scared. Luckily, the first person I met was Charles, and he was so kind."

"Charles was?" I stare at her in surprise and she nods.

"He checked out the bushes and made sure it was safe. Then he could see how shaken I was and arranged for a brandy at the bar. I think he was concerned because he sat with me for a while. I suppose when he saw me in the town, he was worried because once again, I had an argument with Jack and wasn't really thinking straight."

She smiles warmly. "It appears that your husband was my knight in shining armour twice in a row and I'm grateful for it."

"And your husband, is everything ok now?"

"Not really." She looks so devastated I hold my breath because this could be the moment everything changes for me.

"He told me something that has shattered me. You see, Evelyn, unlike you, the thing I want most in life is a baby. To raise a family with my husband who, despite his treatment of me, I love with all my heart. It's why I don't want the business, the distraction from what I really want, but he told me last night he couldn't have children for medical reasons."

"I'm so sorry." My heart fills with compassion for the petite woman who doesn't look as if she has a bad bone in her body, and she smiles through watery tears. "It's fine, I'll get over it, but it's too raw at the moment."

She brushes the tears from her eyes and smiles bravely. "I'm sure we'll work something out because I'm a great believer in fate and this is just another hurdle to jump. It will be the same for you. Things will work out for the best, we just don't know what fate has in store for us, and it will all be fine in the end."

She smiles and then laughs softly. "Anyway, I don't know about you, but I can feel my skin shrivelling up from all this heat. Maybe I need a swim to cool off." She leaves the sauna and I sit for a moment, processing what she just told me. How cruel fate is to give me everything she wants with the wrong man? If I could swap places with her, I would in a heartbeat, but it's not as easy as that because it's obvious she adores her husband and who wouldn't? He's an impressive man and now I've met his wife, part of his allure is crumbling because how could he cheat on such a beautiful person as her? If I felt bad before, I feel like evil personified now and vow to steer well clear of Jack for the rest of my stay.

CHAPTER 29

KIM

*E*velyn was so nice and nothing like I thought she'd be. Having now spent time with them both, it feels as if they are heading in different directions.

As I head for my massage, I wonder what Jack's doing. I'm not even sure if he went on the trip. He stormed off after breakfast and by the time I left to come here he hadn't returned.

Bianca directs me to a darkened room, and it's so peaceful in here. It feels tranquil and smells amazing.

As instructed, I hang my robe on the hook on the wall and position myself face down on the bench that has been covered in a towel. The air conditioning cools my heated skin and the smell of sandalwood and eucalyptus calms my spirit. All around the room are lotus blooms that look majestic and beautiful, and I sigh with pleasure.

The soft music lulls me into a state of relaxation that I sorely need, and then I hear the click of the door opening as the masseuse enters the room.

To my surprise, I hear a male voice speaking in a thick

foreign accent as he says deeply, "My name is Fredo, I will be your masseuse."

Strangely, I don't feel uncomfortable about the fact I'm lying naked on a bench with the prospect of a stranger touching my body. In fact, I'm looking forward to it and I laugh to myself as I picture the look on Jack's face if he could see me now.

I feel the oil hit my body and almost groan out loud as he begins to work it into my skin. The scent, the soft lighting and the seductive music relaxes me and it feels so good being manipulated by his strong hands and I am loving every minute of it. No words are needed as I indulge in the ultimate pleasure as I live the dream.

The time passes quickly and I almost fall asleep before I hear the door click shut behind me, signifying the end of the session. Stretching out with contentment, I swing my legs off the bench and feel a sense of calm that wasn't there before. This was just what I needed and as I slip on my robe, I am looking forward to experiencing more of the same.

I am shown back to the pool by Bianca and see the pretty girl I noticed on the ride from the airport. As I take the seat beside her, she smiles. "Hi, I'm Emma."

"Kim."

I settle down and groan. "That massage was amazing. Have you had yours yet?"

"Yes, and to be honest, it was a little embarrassing because I got so turned on."

She winks and I laugh. "Yes, it was quite a sensual one, probably because it was a man."

"Hmm, probably."

She looks around and sighs with contentment. "You know, I'm loving this place. It's doubtful I will ever be the same again."

"Me too. A week just isn't long enough."

We see one of the women walking past and Emma calls out, "Hey, Chloe, how was the mud room?"

"Amazing, have you done that yet?"

"Yes, I'm just waiting for another cocktail, what about you?"

"Massage."

We both groan with appreciation and then laugh as she raises her eyes. "It's good then."

"The best." Emma shouts across the space dividing us. "Word of warning, it's a man who is great with his hands, just saying."

I notice that Chloe's smile dims a little and smile reassuringly. "Honestly, it's amazing. Really good."

She nods and says loudly, "I'll let you know."

As she heads off, Emma watches her go with a troubled look. "Did she look ok to you?"

"A little worried when you mentioned the man."

"Yes, I thought so too, I wonder why?"

"It was probably nothing. Some people feel a bit funny about that. To be honest, I was at first, but as soon as he started massaging that oil in my skin, I forgot my own name, let alone the sex of the person doing it."

"I was pleased it was a man, it would have felt weird if it was a woman."

Emma laughs and I grin. "You make a good point."

She says with interest. "Did you win this competition like me?"

"Yes, how amazing is that? I never normally bother, there are so many of them, but this one looked so inviting I couldn't resist."

"Yes, me too. I saw it loads before I actually bothered to comment. Sometimes I'm like that. They say people see things seven times before they buy. Maybe it's a psychological thing, it becomes more familiar and sets your mind at rest."

"Yes, I was surprised there weren't that many comments though."

"Yes, me too, although sometimes they run several ads for these things."

"You seem to know a lot about it."

I look at Emma with interest and she nods. "I run my own company."

"That's impressive."

"Not really." She laughs a little bitterly. "It's not doing that well as it happens."

"I'm sorry to hear that, what do you do?"

"I bake. Cakes, biscuits, bread, that sort of thing. Mainly I cater for corporate events but they've dried up lately and so I've been targeting smaller restaurants, although that doesn't work because they mainly prepare their own. Business is a little shaky, which is why I was desperate to get away. Ignore the inevitable and postpone actually having to look for a job."

"That's terrible, do you think you'll have to resort to that?"

"Yes, unless…"

I note the spark in her eye as she leans in and whispers, "Unless the extremely hot guy I've met here, makes me an offer I can't refuse."

"Seriously!" I stare at her in surprise and she grins. "Honestly, Kim, this guy is gorgeous. He owns this place as it happens and can't do enough for me."

"He owns this place, that's…"

"Destiny." Emma looks so pleased with herself, I push aside any reservations I have.

"You see, Kim. I've never been lucky in love. When I was at college, I was popular and I attracted all the good-looking guys and quite honestly had a great time there. Maybe that's why I was never interested in settling down with one man. I had my pick of the bunch and I was ruthless in my picking. The trouble is, when college ended and I actually had to work for a living, the man-candy dried up and I found most of my friends had drifted away. Setting up business on my own didn't give me many opportunities to meet the right man and so I have struggled a little, just dabbling in online dating to get me out at night."

"And now."

"Now I've met the dream and I'm not joking; this man ticks all the boxes. But I only have a few more days with him. What if it's like all the others and I'm left to return home with nothing but a delicious memory to keep me warm?"

"Can you swap numbers, arrange to meet again perhaps?"

"Maybe." She looks thoughtful. "He is English and lives there. In fact, he was telling me that now his business is sorted, he's looking for a wife."

"There you go then, he's ripe for the picking."

I smile with encouragement and she nods happily. "Yes, you're right. Strike while the iron's hot and I'll reel my man in. Thanks, Kim, it's been good to chat."

She stands and says ruefully, "Time for my facial, what have you got next?"

"The mud room followed by a facial. I'm expecting miracles though and hope to walk out of here a new woman."

She grins and as we part company, I'm glad I came. That's two women I've met who were good company. I feel rested and am starting to believe that my problems could disappear with just a little time and readjusted goals. Thinking of the two women I met and their situation, reminds me that I'm the lucky one because my husband is everything to me and if the worst thing is we can't have children, then I must support him in that because I married him for a reason, and I can't imagine my life without him in it.

CHAPTER 30

CHLOE

*I*t's fine, he's a professional and does this all the time. Not every man is a predator, and I must calm down. I repeat the words over and over in my head as I make my way to the treatment room and try to breathe deeply as I head inside and note the soft music and flickering candles set up around the room on every surface.

The scent of jasmine fills the air and I take a deep breath.

It's all good, nothing sinister here, just relaxation and pure bliss.

As instructed, I remove my robe and lie face down on the bed and wait for the treatment to begin. It doesn't take long before I hear the click of the door and I immediately tense up.

A low voice with a foreign accent makes me stiffen a little as he says softly, "My name is Fredo, please relax."

I breathe out slowly and feel the warm oil hit my skin, and I must admit it feels so nice. He begins to massage my body and I can't help stiffen up as I feel his hands on me but he whispers, "Relax and let your mind wander to paradise."

I try to do as he says and as he probes my skin with gentle

147

fingers, I allow my body to adjust to his touch. It feels so good, slightly sensual, and now I know what the other girls were so happy about because this is heaven. I'm amazed at how good I feel and my eyes are heavy as I allow my muscles to relax under his skilful hands.

The whole experience is one of pleasure and as he moves lower, I feel a little embarrassed about how turned on I am. I stifle a groan as he massages my buttocks with his strong fingers but I relax into it and push away the thoughts that haunt me at night and decide this is the best therapy for me as I let him work my body like the professional he is.

He says softly, "I am going to place a special lotion on your back that will loosen the tension in your muscles."

I say nothing and wait for the pleasure to begin, and as I feel the warm liquid trickling down my spine, I groan with pleasure. He works it in and even when his hand brushes the swell of my breast, I bite back a groan because I have never in my life been as relaxed as this. His hands massage, tease and titillate and it's the most pleasurable feeling of pure bliss.

I'm not sure how long it takes, but when he leaves, I feel almost disappointed. Sitting up, I swing my legs over the side and shake myself a little. It's as if every part of my body is vibrating with pleasure, and now I can see what all the fuss is about.

Grabbing my robe, I head outside and see Bianca heading towards me smiling.

"Was that good?"

"Amazing, thank you."

She nods and smiles, "Follow me, your facial is planned for thirty minutes' time. Maybe you would like to rest by the pool with a cocktail of juices designed to restore vitality."

"Lead the way."

I follow her to the pool area and see the glamorous

woman swimming a few lengths, and once again, I envy her figure.

As I take my seat, I accept the cocktail gratefully and watch as she leaves the pool and wraps herself in her robe. Bianca calls out, "Evelyn, it's time for your massage."

She catches my eye and I give her the thumbs up.

"Enjoy, it's amazing."

She smiles. "Thanks, I've been looking forward to this."

As I watch her go, I feel quite proud of myself. It may not be much, but I achieved something huge just then, for me, anyway. For the first time in years, I allowed my body to relax with a stranger and there were no nightmares to ruin the experience for me. Maybe this holiday was just what I needed, to put to rest something that should have been dealt with years ago. Even the thought of seeing that sleazy man again makes no difference because that massage has proved something to me. I need to accept my past and not let it affect my future. I don't want to be scared all the time and I want to take charge, so I make a decision. I'm telling John everything and I'm telling him tonight.

CHAPTER 31

EMMA

*L*unch is an interesting one. The four of us are seated at a round table overlooking the pool, and attentive waiters serve us amazing salads as we sit under the shade of a huge white umbrella. The food here is certainly exquisite, and all around me are extremely contented women.

Chloe looks so much better than when I saw her earlier, and she giggles. "I wonder if the men have had a good time."

Kim laughs. "I hope not."

They all giggle and I wonder if this is what married life does to you. Familiarity breeds contempt it seems and yet imagining myself married to Ben, just leaves me with a warm feeling inside. I wonder if that's his end goal. Striking up a relationship and seeing it through to the end. Perhaps he intends on seducing me and then asking me to be his wife. It wouldn't surprise me, after all, he did say that marriage was his next project. Thinking of myself as a potential project as such, doesn't bother me like it should. I'm old enough to know that love is a game of chance. Some win earlier than others, but Ben would certainly be worth the wait. Just imagining this as my life leaves me feeling impatient to get on with it and thinking about the evening ahead, makes me feel warm inside.

"So, Emma, tell us some more about your date tonight."

They all look at me expectantly as Chloe smiles her encouragement.

"Well, I was just thinking about that as it happens."

"I bet you were."

Evelyn grins and I giggle like a schoolgirl.

"I mean, what would you do, what if he wants to get intimate, it's only been two days, should I let him?"

"NO!"

"YES."

Chloe shakes her head, and both Kim and Evelyn nod vigorously. Chloe groans. "Don't get me wrong, part of me thinks you should go for it. After all, opportunities don't normally come around like this, but what if it ends here, on this island? Would you be able to live with that?"

"Probably." I grin at the other women, who look as if they know where I'm coming from.

"Don't get me wrong, Chloe, I'm no vestal virgin, I've been around the block a few times and have needs as much as any man."

Chloe looks resigned and mumbles, "I suppose, although I'm thinking with my mother's hat on. You see, I have a sixteen-year-old daughter who I would be horrified thinking about in your position. Not that I'm comparing you to her, I mean, you are older and more than capable of making the right decision for you, but she's impressionable and would probably make the wrong choice."

"Haven't we all at some point in our lives?"

Evelyn looks a little sad. "How can you learn unless you make mistakes? I've made several over the years and quite honestly, I wish life came with a manual sometimes."

"Or a crystal ball."

Kim sounds pensive, and I wonder about the two women who appear to have life pretty much worked out from where I'm sitting.

"So, given your experiences, what would you suggest for me?"

"Only you can answer that question." Kim smiles.

"If you want to take things further, do so with the understanding that it may not go anywhere. Don't do it hoping for more because if it fizzles out, you will be disappointed in yourself."

Evelyn nods. "Yes, just enjoy the moment and accept that if it leads somewhere, it's a bonus but don't let passion fool you, think about when that passion fades, because it will you know. Maybe not now, not next year even, but somewhere in the future, it will die a slow death if the man you're with is not the right one for you."

She looks so sad it makes us all take a moment, and it's obvious from the looks on the women's faces that they share the same knowledge. Maybe this is what happens. Perhaps the initial excitement does wear off, but at least I would be rich and disillusioned instead of trying to make ends meet and worrying about where the next meal is coming from. I'm guessing Evelyn knows about that because she obviously married money and at least Ben is way more attractive than her husband. Yes, I'm going for it because this relationship could be the goose that lays the golden egg and it would be no hardship because I wasn't lying, Ben is a dream come true.

Once lunch is over, it signifies the end of our pamper morning and I decide to head to the pool for a spot of sunbathing. A couple of the others join me and I see Chloe greet her partner as he calls her over.

It warms my heart to see their obvious pleasure in each other's company, and I hope they do get married one day.

Maybe I can put in a good word for them with Ben. Perhaps he can arrange a wedding at the last minute as an advert for his resort. I feel quite upbeat as I think of suggestions to help his business. Maybe it will reinforce the fact we were meant to be together. I should pull out all the stops because now I have this chance, I must seize it with both hands.

CHAPTER 32

EVELYN

I decide to head to my room after lunch for a siesta. I'm feeling quite tired and just hope Charles isn't there and I can relax on my balcony and get some peace.

As I walk through the marbled hallway, I think back on a pleasant morning. Most surprising of all was Kim. I liked her. Just thinking of what I did with her husband makes me feel terrible and then to my horror, I see the man himself heading my way. I'm not sure what to do because despite the fact I regret what we did, he is still so incredibly attractive, I'm having a hard time doing the right thing in my mind.

He stops just short of me and smiles and just like that, my principles desert me in a haze of lust.

"Hi."

"Hi." I blush and he steps closer.

"It's good to see you."

"You too."

He seems a little lost for words and then whispers, "I'm sorry about the other day, you know, in the town. I ignored you and I'm sorry about that but well, Kim, you know how it is."

"It's fine, I was in the same position."

His gaze lingers for just a fraction and I see regret in his eyes as he says sadly, "I'm sorry things got a little out of hand in the lift, I hope you didn't think badly of me."

I'm surprised and shrug. "Don't be - sorry that is, I loved every minute."

He smiles and it sends a burst of heat through my entire body. For a moment we just stare at one another and I find myself gravitating towards him and I'm surprised when he steps back a little. The hurt must show on my face because he looks apologetic. "Listen, what happened in the lift was a mistake. A spur of the moment bad decision that I've felt guilty about ever since. I know you probably don't believe me but I love my wife and never meant to hurt her. It's just a good thing we never took it further, so let's just put it behind us as a moment of craziness that got out of hand."

"Excuse me!"

I stare at him in disbelief as he shrugs. "Listen, I'm sorry, it was one mistake, a kiss that should never have happened."

"A kiss. Do you really expect me to think of it as just a kiss? We did a lot more than that Jack and for quite some time if I remember."

"What are you talking about?" He looks surprised and I hiss. "Have you got amnesia or something? What about the gym, if I remember rightly, we did a lot more than kiss inside that cupboard? What's the matter, Jack, do you have a selective memory, or just don't want to admit to cheating on your wife twice in the same day?"

"Listen, I don't know what your problem is but…"

"My problem."

He steps away as I stare at him with fury blazing from my eyes. "We had sex, Jack and you enjoyed every minute of it judging by the sounds coming from you. Don't try to deny it because I was there – remember."

Jack looks worried and if anything, I feel used and snarl, "Just fuck off, Jack, guys like you make me sick inside. You got what you wanted and now you're covering your tail. Get out of my way, I never want to see you again."

I make to leave and his hand stops me and he says in disbelief, "It wasn't me, Evelyn, I wasn't near the gym that night. I argued with Kim and went for a walk, ending up in the bar."

A cold feeling seeps through my veins as my world crashes and burns. Turning slowly, I look at him in horror and say weakly, "It wasn't you?"

He looks worried. "I promise on my life, it wasn't me, why do you think it was?"

Closing my eyes, the full horror of my situation hits me. If it wasn't Jack, then who did I have sex with so violently in the cupboard that night?

Somehow, I break away and walk back to my room. Jack doesn't try to stop me and I can't even look him in the eye. As I walk, images of that night return to haunt me. The way he came at me from behind. The hand wrapping around my throat and the whispered husky voice. *'You're a naughty girl.'*

I thought it was Jack. I thought it was what we had arranged. It didn't even occur to me it could be anyone else.

Shame washes over me as I remember what I did. What *he* did because I made it easy for him. The thought of him inside me makes me choke back a sob. I was so incredibly stupid and allowed something to happen that is wrong on every level. I don't doubt Jack for a second. The horror on his face told me everything I needed to know. My heart is racing out of control as I think about who it could have been. Was it Charles, did he follow me and punish me for daring to argue with him? He's been on edge ever since we arrived, something's definitely up with him and I can't put my finger on it.

Frantically, I think of who else it could be. Someone who

works here perhaps, another guest. Surely it wasn't Chloe's husband. He seems so nice, so normal. What about the creepy man I catch staring at me, making me feel uncomfortable under his gaze? A feeling of despair creeps through me as I realise I will probably never know. I doubt I'll be able to look Charles in the eye, because what if it was him? He knows what I did and it would explain his altering mood and the looks he gave Kim. Maybe he saw me in the lift and somehow found out about our plan to meet. It can be the only explanation.

As soon as I reach the room, I'm grateful to find Charles missing. Quickly, I race to the shower and scrub my body hard. I know it's too late, but I can't shift the feeling of his hands on me. The rough way he handled my body and the pleasure it gave him. Thinking back, I was so stupid - I never saw his face. It all added to the mystery, the excitement, and I loved how forbidden it was. I had sex with a stranger – possibly. I feel so dirty, used, and like a cheap whore. Then again, I shouldn't feel any different because in my mind I was unfaithful to my husband and loved every minute of it.

There is that moment when something so shocking happens it takes a moment for your brain to process the information. A few minutes grace while it works it all out, giving you time to sit and breathe. A shocked state of disbelief when the full horror of your situation doesn't quite hit you yet, and that's exactly how Charles finds me. Sitting on the bed, staring at nothing. Trying hard to piece back together the jagged pieces of a broken life.

I hear him come in but I don't look up and he grumbles, "Well, that's a morning I'm never getting back. You know, next time I would rather wrestle sharks than be bored out of my mind, stuck on a boat with the likes of them. Drinking beers and talking about sport, typical stereotypes. You know…"

Suddenly, he stops and I hear a terse, "What the fuck…"

His tone makes me look up and for the first time since I met him, I see Charles looking shell shocked. He has gone red and his breathing is all over the place. I almost think he's having a heart attack as he makes a strange gurgling sound and I say fearfully, "What is it, Charles, what's wrong?"

He holds up his hand and just stares at his phone and an uneasy feeling creeps over me. Does this involve me and what I've done, has someone told him, has he found out?

He says nothing and turns on his heel and heads for the door and I say fearfully, "Charles, you're scaring me, what's happened?"

"Not now, Evelyn, I can't deal with you right now."

He wrenches open the door and leaves, slamming it hard behind him and I'm left staring at the plain wood, feeling my heart rate increase to dangerous levels.

What's happening?

CHAPTER 33

*J*ack finds me lying by the pool and drops a light kiss on my lips. "Hey."

He settles down on the sun lounger next to me, and I wonder what sort of mood he'll be in now. I'm starting to lose track of them, but it appears he had a good morning because he looks rested and content and the smile he gives me settles my heart a little.

He starts rubbing in the sunscreen and says in a low voice, "I'm sorry, Kim."

"Are you?" My voice is cold because the last conversation we had wasn't pleasant and I'm not sure where we stand now.

He nods and whispers, "I've had some time to think and I haven't been fair on you. I've been blaming you for something that's my problem, and all you've done is be the supportive wife that I really don't deserve. If I've made things difficult for you, I apologise, but it's hard for me to deal with sometimes."

"It must be." I sit up and face him and note the emotion in his eyes as he stares at me and says huskily, "I don't want to lose you, darling, you're the best part of me and I couldn't face this on my own."

"Face what?"

"Life, the future, my problems. You're the best thing that ever happened to me and I don't want to lose you."

"Then stop shutting me out, Jack, stop making it hard for me to talk to you. You blow hot and cold and I don't know what side of you I'm dealing with most of the time. If I'm honest, I'm struggling to understand you and yet..." Reaching out, I take his hand and smile. "I love you."

He smiles and once again everything's alright. He's back, the man I fell in love with, who has so many demons inside him, it's difficult to deal with.

He nods and says regretfully, "Forgive me?"

"Of course, I always do."

He grins and I see a little of his arrogance return as he switches back to the cocky man who tramples over my heart on a daily basis.

"So, how was your morning?"

"Lovely, thank you. What about yours?"

"It was ok, I guess. There was only the three of us in the end. That guy over there, John, I think his name was. He seemed quite decent really, he supports Arsenal, so we had that in common at least."

I roll my eyes and he laughs. "Charles was there too; you know he was seriously boring. He wouldn't stop looking at his phone and appeared anxious because he couldn't get a signal. He kept on asking when we were getting back and was brooding on something."

"Maybe he had work to do, I think he's here on business, anyway."

"Oh yes, I forgot you were close."

Jack's mood switches again as he stares at me angrily, and I sigh. "Listen, Charles was there when you were not. When you left me on the beach that night I was upset and when I walked back, I took a different route. I felt as if someone was following me and I got scared. I ran into Charles and he was kind and helped me calm down, got me a brandy and sat with me for a while."

"This is the first I've heard of it. Who was following you?"

"I'm not sure if anyone was, but it felt like it at the time. It was dark, and I was emotional. It was a strange place, and you had stormed off."

He sighs heavily. "So, it was my fault again. It's no wonder we argue, honestly, Kim, I always feel as if you're judging me."

Counting to ten in my mind, I fight the frustration. This is typical Jack, throwing accusations and deflecting the blame onto me.

He lies back on the sun lounger and an uneasy feeling creeps over me. Do I even like him anymore, let alone love him? I'm not sure how I feel because outside of the sexual attraction, I'm not sure if there's anything else.

Looking across at Chloe and John, I see him rub sunscreen on her back and she laughs, the joyous sound carrying across the pool towards me, showing me that companionship, friendship and togetherness are much more important than the physical side of a relationship.

As I lie back on the sun lounger and the warm rays of the sun hit me, I try not to face the fact that my marriage is heading only one way.

LATER THAT AFTERNOON, we head back to our room and Jack is acting as if nothing is wrong. He seems playful in fact as he grabs my hand and talks about his day, but I can't seem to shake my mood at all. Do I even like him anymore? I'm not sure that I do because all I can see in my mind is the side of him I hate.

We notice a board in reception and stop to take a look.

You are invited to a champagne reception tonight at 8pm in the bar.

"Sounds good, this place could do with livening up."

Jack seems quite upbeat and grasps my hand tightly. "It's been a while since we had a night out. Should be good."

"Yes, it should."

We carry on walking to our room and he says huskily, "Let me make it up to you, darling, you know I'm better showing rather than telling."

He winks, and it strikes me that he's probably right. He's never been good with words, using them more to inflict pain than to reassure, and yet in bed he's always been a master. Maybe this is what we both need, the intimacy that the physical side of a relationship creates, so I nod. "I can't wait."

However, as we stumble into the room and Jack pulls me in for a deep kiss, this time it feels as if I'm going through the motions because this is just sex. It's meaningless because there's no substance to our relationship. There is actually nothing else, no shared dreams, no sense of a future with a family and the pleasure that gives you. No common goal other than sex and then separate lives. I don't want this anymore and I'm not sure if I want him either because I am fast realising you can actually love and hate someone at the same time but will I be strong enough to walk away and where will I go?

CHAPTER 34

CHLOE

*I*t's good to have John back by my side. He obviously had a good time because he's playful and rested and seems less tense. After a lovely couple of hours sunbathing, we decide to go for a walk on the beach and it feels good holding his hand with the soft breeze from the ocean cooling our heated skin.

I feel more relaxed than I have in a long time, and even my daily call home did little to dampen my spirits.

However, my mood changes quickly when I see the man from the town heading towards us. My heart rate increases as we pass and I grip John's hand tightly as he nods and says a polite, "Hi."

The man stops and my heart sinks as he says loudly, "Hey, how are you enjoying your stay?"

John replies because I can't even look at him. "It's good thanks, are you?"

"Yeah, it's one amazing place, although I thought there'd be more people, it's a little like a ghost town with just a few of us rattling around."

John nods "Nice though. Did you win the holiday, like most of us?"

"Yeah, it surprised me, in a good way though."

I feel his eyes roaming up and down my body and I shiver a little as John says, "I never saw you on the boat, didn't you fancy it?"

"Not really, boats aren't my thing."

"It was good, just a few of us and a crate of beers and nothing to do but relax. It's not something I do every day, so I was keen to try it."

"Sounds good. No, I was content just hanging around the resort."

Once again, I shiver inside as I hold John's hand tightly because there's something about this man that causes my nerves to stand to attention. The fact John is being so friendly has me screaming inside because if he knew what that man said to me, he would probably be punching him right now. It's why I never said anything in the first place because John has a temper I try my hardest to keep under control. He scares me when he loses it, and I do everything in my power to keep it hidden.

I tune out of their conversation as I think of the last time John lost it. It was stupid really, an argument with a man over a parking space. Road rage of the worst kind and we were just lucky there was nobody around to witness the fact that John punched the guy to the ground. It was an overreaction of the worst kind because the guy had only stolen his parking space and I watched in horror as John stormed out of the car and approached the man as he locked up. They argued and the next thing I knew, John slammed him against his car and punched him in the stomach. The man fell to the ground and John kicked him hard. I remember screaming at him and he just wandered back to the car and got in as if nothing had happened, telling me to stop moaning, before driving away.

I have never forgotten that incident, and for a while it made me doubt my decision to be with him at all. But I was pregnant and madly in love, but I have never forgotten how volatile he can be.

If John knew what this man had said to me, I'm in no doubt he would be tasting sand right now and John would probably be arrested. So, I keep it to myself, like I do most things and just tune out of their conversation.

Luckily, it doesn't last long and as we walk away, John says in a low voice, "There's something weird about that man."

"I agree."

He shakes his head. "Who comes to a place like this on their own? He didn't even come on the boat, surely he was meant to as part of the deal."

"Maybe he doesn't see it like that."

"Well, if you ask me, he should be told. It's the least we can do, test out everything for them when they've gone to a lot of trouble to make this a good experience and they deserve our cooperation."

"I agree."

He squeezes my hand. "So, how was your morning, you seem quite chilled for the first time in ages?"

"It was amazing, the other women were nice, and it was good to relax and forget about the stress of life being a mother throws at you."

"You shouldn't let them get to you."

"How can I not? I worry about them, it's a cruel world out there and they're living in one I don't really understand. They could be exposed to all sorts of dangers that we don't even know about. You hear about it all the time; the cyber world is a dark place and I wouldn't know how to even access it."

"They're fine, honestly, Chlo, you really should relax, they're more switched on than you think."

"Are they, I'm not so sure?"

"Well, you're not doing them any favours pandering to them and you should just chill a little and let them make their own mistakes, it's the only way they'll learn."

"You're wrong about that, John."

I hold my breath as he laughs, "I doubt it."

"You are, you see, even the most careful person can be a target and have no control of it all."

"What are you talking about, it doesn't make sense, what do you know, anyway?"

"John, I…"

The words catch in my throat as my past invades my present, battling to be heard.

"Chloe, what's wrong?"

Maybe it's the concern in his voice, or the fact he seems so chilled, I say with a sob, "There's something I should tell you; it may make you understand why I'm so protective."

He grips my hand tighter and says evenly, "I'm listening."

"Can we sit down?" He nods, looking concerned, and pulling me down to the sand, on the edge of the ocean, he wraps his arm around my shoulders.

I stare out to sea and say with a slight hesitation, "It happened when I was eighteen. I went on a night out with my friends to a club in town, you know, the usual thing back then. Well, to cut a long story short, my drink was spiked without me even realising it."

John tenses up beside me and I say quickly, "I felt as if I was going to be sick and went to the toilets but I never made it. I was dragged outside and…"

I break off as out of nowhere, the tears fall and I put my

head in my hands and cry as if my heart just broke. John places his arm around my shoulders and pulls me close and his next words shock me more than anything, "I know."

"You know." I turn and stare at him in confusion and he says sadly, "It's ok, Chloe, you don't have to tell me because I already know what happened?"

"But how? I never told you."

"It was your mum. When we got together, she pulled me aside one day. I think you were working, and I dropped around on the off chance. We had quite the conversation, and she said if I was serious about you, I needed to know."

"She never said – *you* never said – why?"

"Because she asked me not to say anything. She told me how traumatic it had been and that you couldn't talk about it. She wanted me to know, so I could deal with any problems as they arose and understand if you found certain situations difficult to deal with."

"She really told you, I don't understand."

He smiles sadly. "You're a lot like your mum, Chloe. You take everyone's problems and make them yours. I see it with the girls. You will do anything for them and fight their corner when they are in the wrong. I understand your need to protect them and just thinking of them experiencing what you went through, makes my blood run cold."

"Why didn't you tell me you knew?"

"Why didn't you tell me yourself? Because it was easier not to. To keep something hidden that brought you pain; to forget it ever happened and not let it affect our lives. It needed to come from you, Chloe, because it's your past to deal with."

He smiles so sweetly it brings tears to my eyes as he says softly, "We all have things in our past we would rather forget. You know, I may have my own fair share of them." He laughs and I nod through my tears, "I can think of a few."

He rubs my shoulder and drops a light kiss on my lips. "I suppose, we have been guilty of bottling things up and not trusting each other with our emotions. I can never begin to imagine how you felt after what happened to you, it's the worst kind of crime and something I will never understand. I want to be a man you can trust with your darkest thoughts, the man who will take your problems and make them go away. I want to be strong for you, Chloe, and not make you feel as if you have to hide things from me but I struggle with the words sometimes and know I have my own demons to control. I want to be that person, Chlo, but you need to let me."

I feel a little ashamed that I never trusted him with this before, when all along he knew every sordid detail. Then there's my mum, telling him something that was my secret to reveal. Would I do the same to one of my daughters, interfere in a relationship that could have backfired and made him walk away? As I think about mum, my heart breaks because now I'm a mother myself, I know how painful that must have been for her. I shut her out and retreated into my shell and became emotionless and cold. She was so worried about me and I pushed her away. I feel ashamed of how I treated the one person who always had my best interests at heart, and as John's arms wrap around me and pull me close, I break down in his arms.

Suddenly, it's as if the cloud has lifted and the sun has broken through because he has stepped up and become the man I always wanted and I'm only just realising that he has been all the time.

CHAPTER 35

EMMA

*T*he reflection staring back at me is full of determination and I almost don't recognise myself as I stare at a woman who has only one thing on her mind. Ben.

Speaking with the girls has given me a sense of purpose. I need to make this work; to make Ben fall in love with me because I want what they have, but I want more. Ben can give that to me and the fact he's so easy on the eye makes him even more desirable. So tonight's the night. I will make Ben fall so hard he won't recover, and I picture the desire in his eyes when he sees the sexy lingerie caressing my body and smooth down the tight black dress that I purposefully chose for this evening. Tossing back my freshly washed hair, I blink at my reflection through the fake eyelashes I'm wearing that make my eyes look sexy and sultry and as I look around the room, I pray I don't end up back here alone tonight.

The knock at the door makes my heart quicken and taking a deep breath, I open it and see him waiting, looking so desirable I feel the lust tearing through me. He is so sexy, so cool and dangerous for my heart because he looks good enough to eat.

He stares at me with dark intention and I smile. "Hi."

Holding out his hand, he smiles. "You look beautiful, Emma."

His eyes travel the length of my body with an appreciation that makes me happy inside, and as my fingers close around his, I take a step towards my future.

"Where are we going?"

"There's a restaurant on the top of the hill I like to go to, it's a little off the beaten track but popular with the locals."

"It sounds nice."

He leads me through the reception and waves to the receptionist who looks at me with envy and I feel quite smug as I smile in her direction.

We make our way outside and he flicks the key fob and bright headlights beckon us over to a smart red sports car that looks like something James Bond would drive and as he holds open the passenger door and I slide onto the cool leather seats; I feel as if I've come home. This all feels like destiny to me, and I'm excited for the future.

Ben jumps in beside me and we are soon tearing through the streets and I look around with interest at a place that appears worlds away from England. The heat, the lack of buildings and wide-open spaces, seem a million miles away from the towns I usually explore.

"What made you choose to build your hotel here?" I start my campaign by showing an interest in his business and he says brightly, "It came on the market and I booked the first flight available to check it out. I've always wanted to build a luxury resort, and this was as good a place as any. It screams paradise, and the land was cheap. The airport is close by but not close enough to destroy the peace and it's easy to get here."

"Do you have any other hotels?"

I am keen to know more about this man and he shakes his head. "No, I invest in companies, tech ones mainly, but I wanted to build something substantial for once, to have something tangible to show for my money, instead of just an entry on my asset spreadsheet."

"You obviously have a talent for business if you can afford to do things like this."

"I do."

He switches the conversation and says evenly, "Tell me about your business, what are your plans?"

"I'm not sure?" I shrug. "It's not really paying the bills, and so I was thinking of a change of direction. Maybe look for a job somewhere – I don't suppose you have any going?"

I giggle and he nods. "Probably, I could put you in touch with the HR department, see if there's something suitable."

"Oh, thanks." To be honest, the last thing I want to do is become one of his employees, I have a much better idea in mind and as we pull up outside a small restaurant, I say flirtatiously, "You certainly know how to make a girl's head spin."

The fairy lights twinkle over the front of the building and flaming torches guard the entrance, casting a romantic glow across the deserted hilltop.

He turns and his eyes sparkle in the darkness as he says slightly huskily, "There's a reason I want to make your head spin, Emma."

"Is there?" I lick my lips and lean a little closer and inhale the musky scent of a desirable man. "Well, for your information, you have succeeded."

He leans closer and our lips touch briefly as he whispers, "I wonder if you know just how much I want this. You - this situation, for you to fall deeply in love with me."

My breath hitches as I fall deep and hard, and as his lips

crush against mine, I dance a victory parade in my head. He wants the same - he wants *me*.

Ben kisses like he means business and I'm loving every minute of this. The sense of new beginnings, of starting something that will end so well for me and the culmination of a plan that will deliver me what I want. He makes my head spin with it all; his good looks, his devastating wealth, and his enigmatic personality. He is everything I wanted in life and searched so hard to find and as he pulls me closer, I demonstrate just how much I want him – to share his life and never leave.

Reluctantly, he pulls back and sighs. "Come, we should eat something."

Food is actually the furthest thing from my mind as we head inside the dimly lit restaurant that looks out across the darkened hillside.

We are shown to an intimate table overlooking the view, and as the sun sets in the sky, it casts a magical glow over the evening.

The waiter arrives and serves us a bottle of champagne that is chilling in a bucket beside the table, and I raise my eyes. "You've planned this already."

He nods and smiles wickedly. "I have it all worked out."

He raises his glass to mine and as they touch, he whispers, "To realising your dream."

"I'll second that."

As we clink glasses and I take a sip of the cool liquid that slides down my throat, I feel as if I have arrived. Finally, everything is working out for me. It no longer matters that the business is failing because I am winning at life right now, and as I throw Ben a sexy look, I can just imagine the pleasure that is heading my way this evening.

CHAPTER 36

EVELYN

*C*harles was gone so long I thought I'd have to call out a search party, although I was relieved to have some time alone to deal with the shock.

It wasn't Jack.

I still can't wrap my head around that. I was so certain. It was what I wanted, of course it was, but if I'd have known it was someone else, it would have been a very different story.

I almost think I'm going to have to dine alone, but Charles returns when I'm applying the finishing touches to my make-up.

He seems angry and looks worried, and I immediately know something is very wrong.

"Is everything ok, Charles?"

He groans and sits on the chair with his head in his hands. "Not really."

"Do you want to talk about it?"

"No. Not with you, anyway."

"What's that supposed to mean?" My heart is beating wildly inside me as he stares into space. "I need to see Ben, it's urgent."

"Is that where you've been?"

"For god's sake, Evelyn, I'm trying to think. Stop asking me stupid questions and try to pretend you even care."

He stands and heads for the shower. "I'm getting changed, we should eat and attend that stupid champagne reception. Apparently, Ben will be there, something about launching the resort officially. I'll grab a moment with him then."

He slams the door behind him and I try to shrug it off because it wouldn't be the first time Charles has let business affect him. When it's all good, he walks around with a smug smile on his face. He's always been pompous, and I hate it when he's obviously gloating about something. It usually involves an expensive present for me, presented in full view of a packed restaurant, demonstrating to the masses how lucky I am to have landed a catch like him. Then I'm usually subjected to a night of his attention that usually ends with him falling asleep, leaving me feeling used as always.

Increasingly, I am coming to the conclusion that I am just another possession to him. Not worthy of deep conversation and just an object, styled to perfection to complement his lifestyle.

I was never that woman. I always wanted a career; to make my mark and yet I fell in love with the first man who showed me some attention and when Charles wants something, he pulls out all the stops to get it.

WE HEAD DOWNSTAIRS for dinner and notice the other couples are already here. I can't even look at Jack as we stop by their table and Charles makes brief polite conversation. I can tell he's uptight, I've lived with him long enough to recognise the signs and so I say little and just concentrate on eating my food and drinking way more than I should.

Luckily Charles is preoccupied, which gives me time to think about my situation. As I eat, I look around at the tables and wonder about the people who sit there. Chloe and her partner are probably the happiest ones here. He is laughing at something she says and occasionally reaches out and grasps her hand tightly.

I can't even look at Jack but notice Kim appears on edge and is just staring gloomily out to sea, while Jack appears to be studying his watch and drinking more than is good for him. Then there's the solitary man who is staring around him with interest. He catches my eye, and a shiver passes through me. There's something evil lurking beneath his skin because it's all there in that one look as our eyes connect and I feel as if he's stripping me bare.

My mouth dries and I taste bile as I contemplate that I've found the man responsible. It's the way he looks at me, knowing, conniving, and as if he's doing dirty things to me in his mind. He raises his glass to me in a mock salute and I look away, the blood draining from my face as I grasp the stem of the wine glass and chuck the contents back in one go.

Charles grumbles, "Steady on, I don't want an alcoholic wife to deal with as well as everything else."

His words sound bitter and make my blood boil and I say sharply, "What's going on, what is your problem?"

"Just shut the fuck up and let me think for a moment."

I stare at him in shock as he taps on his phone and looks more worried than I've ever seen him.

He sighs with exasperation. "For god's sake, will this never end, where is that man?"

"Mr Wheeler?"

"Yes."

He looks around him and I see a bead of sweat on his upper lip that surprises me. Charles doesn't sweat – ever.

Not in the heat, not after sex, certainly not during it because you'd have to exert yourself for that. His idea is to lie back and let me do all the work, before spinning me around and pounding me mercilessly until he reaches his own happy ending and just hopes I make it there under my own steam.

Maybe that's why I got carried away. It was the most passionate encounter of my life, so it's no wonder I'm feeling crushed. Once again, I catch the eye of the man across the restaurant and see the interest in his expression as he looks at me. Maybe he thinks I'm of the same mind, thinks he's pulled as they say, so I pointedly lower my eyes and look away. It's got to be him, surely, but if it's not, who could it be?

In my mind I know it's not Charles, he's just not capable of it. Jack has also made it pretty clear it wasn't him. Could it be Chloe's partner, or someone who works here? My mind goes around in circles and I'm delirious with regret. I have a very bad feeling that a storm's approaching and as I look out on the balmy night sky, I know it won't be due to the weather.

CHAPTER 37

KIM

I'm grateful when the meal ends and we leave the table to head into the bar for the champagne reception. It's hard trying to make conversation with a man I am increasingly finding it difficult to understand what I ever saw in him. Maybe he smashed my rose-coloured spectacles when he pulled away from me because now I'm seeing this marriage differently. He's so cold one minute and intensely hot the next. One minute he wants me and in the next wants his space. Then there's the fact he can't have children. Maybe that's what's tearing him up inside but not to even talk about it. How can we possible move forward until we address the issue?

I thought I would love this holiday, and I was super excited to be here at all. Now I only want to go home and refocus. I need to reassess my life plan because this isn't what I had in mind. I want it all, to be one half of a couple who want the same things. To share the same dreams and love one another wholeheartedly, despite what happens to knock them down.

Jack slips his arm around my waist and beams at Chloe

and her partner. "John, mate, have you recovered from earlier?"

"Yes, it was quite a morning."

Chloe drags me to the side and grins. "Men! You know John really enjoyed spending time with Jack. Apparently, Evelyn's husband was in a right old mood and spent most of his time on the phone."

I nod. "Yes, Jack told me he was preoccupied."

"Evelyn looks as if she's struggling. Should we rescue her?"

I look across and seeing the misery on Evelyn's face, my heart goes out to her. Chloe's right, she does seem upset about something. A loud laugh comes from beside us, and Chloe raises her eyes and whispers. "Men are worse than women. John has found a kindred spirit in Jack in more ways than one."

"What do you mean?"

I smile and look at my husband laughing with John and I must admit he does seem happy and Chloe grins. "They share more than just a love of Arsenal and a vasectomy operation in common. I've never seen John so relaxed with someone he's just met."

"I'm sorry, what did you say?"

I think I must have misheard and Chloe shrugs, "I've never seen John so..."

"No, before that, their common interests."

"You mean the love of Arsenal and comparing vasectomies. John told me Jack's went a lot more smoothly than his, poor man."

I don't know how I carry on standing as I look across at Jack sharply. Vasectomy, what the hell?

Chloe drags me across to Evelyn and I fight back the tears. Jack had a vasectomy - since when?

When you think about it, words can break your heart, or

they can change your day, and in this moment as Chloe's words settle around me like the fallout from a devastating missile attack, I know those words have changed everything.

I almost can't concentrate as Evelyn looks up in relief as we join her. Chloe, luckily, seems quite upbeat and does most of the talking, "This is nice; maybe we will get to meet the famous Ben who owns this place. I'm guessing that's where Emma is now; I didn't see her at dinner."

"No, she was definitely not here."

Chloe looks at Evelyn sharply as her face falls and whispers, "Is everything ok?"

Despite my own personal shock, I can definitely see something is up and Evelyn's eyes fill with tears as she whispers, "Do you know who that man is?"

We follow her gaze and I see the single man watching us with an interested expression and to my surprise, Chloe shivers and looks as if she's got a bitter taste in her mouth. "He scares the life out of me."

"What, that man, why?"

From the look in their eyes, they have something I need to know and Chloe whispers, "Listen, I haven't said anything to John but when we were in Kurraga on that trip, he came and spoke to me when John was in the toilet.

"What did he say?"

From the look on her face, it's not a pleasant memory and she shudders. "He gave me his key card and told me to meet him in his room. He was frightening and told me I was to blame for tempting him with lustful looks and giving him the eye."

"You are kidding me, that's disgusting." I stare at her in shock and then at him, and he laughs before turning away. I think back to when I thought someone was following me and remember him passing us and heading this way and I say in a worried voice, "You know, I did feel something strange on

179

the first night. It felt as if someone was following me. I was quite scared really and come to think of it, I saw him on the beach just a little while before."

For some reason, Evelyn looks even worse and I feel uncomfortable when I think of the time I spent with her husband that night. I was lucky he was on hand by the sounds of it and Chloe says with concern, "Are you ok, Evelyn?"

She appears to shake herself and smiles briefly. "I think I've had too much sun; I feel a little faint."

Chloe looks at me and I can tell she doesn't believe a word of it but before we can probe any deeper, Charles heads across and whispers, "Ben's arrived, I'm going to have a word."

We watch him leave and Chloe says with interest, "Is that the man Emma told us about?"

Evelyn nods. "The owner of this resort. Apparently, he's some kind of super investor and whatever he touches turns to gold."

"You know, I was wondering why there are so few of us this week." Chloe looks thoughtful.

"Don't you think it's odd that he would test out the facilities on just a handful of people? I'm not going to lie, I've enjoyed the space, but it does feel a little eerie, don't you agree?"

I nod because the thought has crossed my mind a thousand times already.

Evelyn nods. "It's certainly the first trip I've ever been on like this. Charles doesn't normally mix business with pleasure, and I wonder what's so urgent that he needs to speak to Ben now. He's been worrying about something all day."

Chloe nods. "John told me the same. He didn't enjoy the boat trip at all and was annoyed there was no signal. Maybe he shouldn't have gone on the boat."

"Maybe, then again, Charles does like to experience five star living and the boat certainly offered that."

I see Jack heading my way and feel physically sick.

He lied to me.

When he said he couldn't have children, I didn't know it was because he *chose* not to. I'm not sure if I will ever forgive him if it was through choice, rather than for medical reasons. I suppose I will have to confront him about it later, but for now I turn and say brightly, "Well, let's just enjoy ourselves regardless. Who fancies a cocktail?"

Chloe and Evelyn nod and we head towards the bar, leaving Jack trailing behind us, looking a little put out by the cold shoulder.

He's seen nothing yet.

CHAPTER 38

EMMA

I am living the dream. I can't even put into words how happy I am right now, and as we pull up at the resort, I am hoping Ben whisks me straight to his room to seal the deal. Dinner was amazing, the company was incredible, and I have fallen deeply in love with everything that goes with Ben Wheeler.

As he parks up and heads around to open my door like the true gentleman he is, I practice my new name. Emma Wheeler, Mrs Benjamin Wheeler, wife of the millionaire that every woman wants in her bed and on her arm. It's obvious he's chosen me to be that woman if the loaded looks and whispered promises are anything to go by.

All through dinner, Ben spoke of his dreams for the future. Marriage, babies, several houses all around the world and a life spent in luxury. He painted a very desirable picture, one I am keen to feature in, and all the time he spoke, he gazed deeply into my eyes and reeled me in.

My heart is singing as I take his hand and step from the sports car and he kisses it gallantly and whispers, "We should stop by the champagne reception, I have an important speech to make."

"Do we have to?"

Shifting closer, I wrap my hand around the back of his head and pull him in for a kiss because I am desperate to stake my claim to this man once and for all.

To my surprise, he pulls back and takes my hand, saying firmly, "We must, as I said, it's important and business must come before pleasure."

He winks and drags me behind him and I push down my disappointment. He's right, this is his business and I must be mindful of that, so I head inside, looking forward to seeing the expressions on everyone's faces when they see me walking in with him.

As soon as we step into the bar, I see Evelyn's husband heading our way with a worried look on his face and Ben laughs softly beside me. "Emma, darling, maybe you should go and find your friends and watch from there. Make sure you grab a glass of champagne to toast the success of the resort, it's going to be quite some party."

Feeling a little annoyed that I must watch from the side-lines, instead of by his side so I can gloat about my prize catch, I just nod and smile sexily, "Don't be long, I'm anxious to be alone with you."

As I head off, I hear Charles say urgently, "Ben, we really need to talk, what the hell is this text all about?"

Tuning out, I head towards my friends who crowd around looking curious.

"Wow, Emma, he's gorgeous."

Chloe is the first to speak and I can't help the smug look

that has appeared to settle permanently on my face. "Yes, he is rather."

Kim smiles sweetly, "I think you make a lovely couple; I hope you'll be very happy."

"You know, Kim, I think we will. He's already talking marriage and babies; I think he wants four, but I'm going to stop at one. I need to free up my time to enjoy my new life after all, wouldn't you agree, Evelyn?"

"What, oh yes, you make a lovely couple."

I stare at her in surprise and I notice that Chloe shakes her head and Kim looks worried. Something has definitely happened and I wonder if it's got something to do with Charles, who is gesticulating frantically to Ben, who just smiles as he looks at the people around him. As I watch, I see him put his hand on Charles's arm and say something that makes Charles annoyed by the look on his face and then Ben moves away, leaving him glaring after him.

Evelyn sighs. "Maybe their business deal has gone wrong. Charles has a knack for messing things up."

"Surely not, Ben didn't look worried." I feel anxious because I hope he's not about to lose any money just when I've arrived to spend it. That would be just my luck.

Suddenly, I hear Ben's voice coming across loud and clear as he holds a microphone and there's a sudden hush in the room.

"Ladies and gentlemen, may I introduce myself. My name is Ben Wheeler and I am the owner of Lotus Lake Resort and Spa. Firstly, I would like to welcome you all and extend my gratitude for your help in testing out the facilities. I hope they are to your liking."

There's a gentle murmur around the room and I notice there is quite a crowd gathering. It appears the staff have joined us and I look with interest at the chefs, waiters, receptionists and maids. In fact, it appears there is quite a crowd and I feel so proud of what he has accomplished.

I notice that someone is rolling down a huge projector screen and wonder what we're about to see because it's obvious Ben is keen to show us something. Maybe it's the building process of this lovely resort. I certainly hope so. It will be interesting to see how it evolved.

Ben smiles and laughs softly and appears to be enjoying himself. "Well, Lotus Lake is the end product of a dream I had as a child. You see, I was born into poverty, not the huge wealth that I enjoy now."

I smile at my friends with that smug look that just won't go away and listen to him tell everyone how lucky I am.

"Yes, I started out in a hostel with my mother, who struggled terribly. We were soon housed by the council but never had any money, sometimes even for food. Life was hard, and yet she did her best. She struggled to look after herself, let alone me, and I was always the child that never had enough to eat and wore donated clothes."

I feel a surge of pity as I think of the boy this amazing man once was and think about my own loving childhood. I can't begin to imagine what it must have been like for him, but he obviously had some luck along the way, so I listen as he carries on.

"Things never improved, and when my mother fell ill, I was put into care."

Kim gasps beside me and I'm surprised to see tears rolling down her face as she looks at him with pity. It annoys me a little because this man should be admired, not pitied, and I frown a little.

"Luckily, I was adopted by an amazing couple when my mother lost her fight with cancer and although it was hard, they made me into the man I am today. Unfortunately, they couldn't be here this week but they arrive on Monday and I will only be too happy to show them what I have achieved with their love and encouragement."

He pauses and I see a look of distaste pass across his face as he looks at the man who appears to be on his own. "However, I am lucky to have one member of my family here to see how far I've come. A man who abandoned me as a child and denied my mother the money to raise her son and put food on the table. A man who couldn't have cared less and wanted nothing to do with the child he created."

I think I stop breathing as the man blinks and looks at Ben in astonishment as Ben waves his hand towards him. "Let me introduce Ray Baker. The scumbag who deserted his own wife and child because he found someone else. The man who resisted all my efforts to contact him and the man I hate with a passion. Well, daddy dearest, who's laughing now?"

All eyes turn to the man, who stares at Ben in horror. He shakes his head in disbelief as Ben snarls, "I've learned a lot about you over the years and was curious to discover it for myself, which is why I rigged the competition to bring you here. I guessed you wouldn't have come if you knew I was here, so surprise, daddy, meet your son. However, the more I learned of you, the more I hated you, if that was at all possible."

There is not a sound in the room as a family drama plays out right before our eyes and Ben says roughly. "I brought you here to thank you. If you hadn't been such a bad father, I would never have had the ambition or the drive to succeed that I have today. As a kid, it's difficult to understand why your father doesn't want you. Turned your back on you and left you with nothing. All the other kids at school had someone to look up to. They had loving homes and enough to eat, the latest toys and decent clothes. I had regrets. Regrets that my father didn't love me. I blamed myself, I blamed my mother, I blamed God. But I *never* blamed you. I thought it was my fault you left. You didn't love me, and I thought that for some time. When I used to lie awake in bed hearing my mother crying herself to sleep, I prayed to God that you would somehow hear her and come and save us. To step up and be the father I wanted you to be. You never came. The older I got, the more I missed you. Someone to look up to; to teach me what being a man involved. You weren't there."

He stops and I can almost taste the emotion in the air as his voice shakes a little.

"When mum died, I was left alone and scared. I had already been adopted by the kindest people I had ever met, but I still visited her in the hospice. You broke her, you broke me, but when someone hits rock bottom, the only way is up. I was never ashamed to be broken because I used the pain it left me with to build myself back up stronger and into the man you see before you today."

Kim is openly crying beside me and even I have a tear in my eye as everyone's attention is riveted on the man purging his soul to a man who obviously couldn't care less.

Ben stands strong and unwavering as he says softly, "The name of this resort is not by chance. My new parents taught me many things, but the thing I identified with the most was Buddhism. You see, it resonated with me when it taught me that ultimately, I was in control of my fate. You learn from the past to shape your future, and the symbol of the lotus flower was the most powerful image of all. It grows from the mud, the dirt, and emerges resplendent in its breath-taking beauty. It's a symbol of purity, self-regeneration, and spiritual enlightenment. I chose the lotus flower because I identify with it. I grew from the mud and the dirt, and I have created something beautiful. So, you see, Ray, you created something beautiful, but you weren't interested in that, so what can I say, Karmas a bitch because now you can see what could have been yours to share. So, I hope you take this image home with you, back to your seedy life spent preying on defenceless women, and remember that the child you never wanted, never wants to see you again. You're dead to me."

He stares at him in disgust and snarls, "Now get the hell out of my fucking resort."

Ray makes to speak but Ben turns away and I watch as two burly security guards haul him backwards and almost drag him from the room, shouting, "I'm sorry, son, let me explain."

Chloe shivers beside me and Kim is wiping her eyes furiously as Ben turns and says evenly.

"Please forgive me, that was a long time coming."

He appears to compose himself and then says roughly, "If you'd like to refresh your drinks, we will take a short break."

As he makes his way out of the room, the silence follows him.

CHAPTER 39

CHLOE

I am destroyed. That was intense, and I feel so emotional as I look after the man who just bared his soul in public. Emma appears lost for words and looks at us in shock. "What just happened?"

Kim sniffs. "That was devastating, I feel so sorry for him."

"Who, Ray?"

Emma looks astonished as Kim snaps, "No, Ben, of course. I can't believe he put himself through that, the poor man."

"He's hardly poor." Emma shakes her head and at this moment in time, I really despise Emma.

Evelyn shivers. "I knew there was something shady about that man, he had an evil aura."

Kim nods. "I felt it too. Well, at least he's gone now."

Emma grabs a glass of champagne from a passing waiter and drinks it quickly. "Well, that was unexpected."

We look up as Evelyn's husband Charles heads our way and says angrily, "That man is so slippery. I tried to get a moment, but he pushed me aside. I deserve more respect than that. We have business to discuss."

"For goodness's sake, Charles, the man just poured his heart out, give him a break for a minute."

Evelyn looks angry and Charles snarls, "This affects you too you stupid woman, I don't think you realise how serious this is."

"How dare you?"

Evelyn is quivering with rage and it feels uncomfortable to watch and so we all make our excuses. "Um, I think I should catch up with John."

Emma says loudly, "I should really go and see if Ben needs me."

Kim nods "I should just, um… well… yes…"

One by one, we all drift away and I hear raised voices as we go.

As soon as I reach John, I raise my eyes. "My goodness, that was so intense."

He nods. "Poor guy, it sounds like he had a miserable childhood."

"Hm, he did well though, those new parents are obviously worth more than gold. He was lucky."

John slips his arm around my shoulders and to my surprise, he leans down and kisses me long and hard in full view of everyone. Feeling a little embarrassed, I pull back and whisper, "What was that for?"

"For taking you for granted. For not making an honest woman of you and for not being the man you deserve."

"But you are."

His eyes soften and he strokes my face lightly. "I want to be. I want to make an honest woman of you, Chloe. I want us to share the same name and commit to one another. I don't want any regrets in our lives, and it's taken me coming here to realise that. We only get one shot at life and now we're away from our kind of normal, I want to return and turn a new page and write a different future."

"But how, we can't afford it?"

"We will make it work even if we head down to the registry office one day and have takeaway fish and chips on the seafront afterwards. I don't care how we do it, how much money we spend, I just want you."

I am reeling as John offers me something I have wanted for so long I never actually thought it would happen and as I fall into his outstretched arms and they wrap around me, I don't think I've ever been so happy.

However, it's that moment I think back on because happiness, as it turns out, can be just a fleeting moment and then we hear a loud, "May I have your attention?"

We look up to see Ben has returned and appears to have composed himself and a hush falls over the room.

"Forgive me, I just needed a moment. I never realised how emotional that delivery would be. It felt good though."

There's a small cheer that goes up from his staff and he laughs. "Anyway, where were we?"

He looks around the room and I see his gaze fall on me and my heart rate quickens as I sense something is not quite right. He smiles, and it seems so sad, it brings tears to my eyes and as he looks away, I watch him stare at Jack and notice a hard-edge creep into his expression.

"As it turns out, there's another person here who I wanted to share in my success. A man I knew from school, someone who was popular, a bit of a bully and a guy everyone wanted to be on the right side of."

He looks quite angry as he points at Jack. "I'm surprised you don't remember me, Jack. Admittedly I've grown up a lot since Greendale but we were in the same class at school. I suppose the beard and glasses change a person, also the clothes are a lot more expensive than I used to wear."

Jack looks confused, and then the penny drops along with his mouth. "I remember you."

191

Ben nods. "That's right, you bullied the hell out of me for my entire school life at Greendale. You beat me, stole my lunch, belittled and taunted me and made my life miserable in every way. I actually hated you back then and thought of a thousand ways I could get my revenge, but how could I? I was a boy with nothing and you had everything. Good looks, popularity, and the life I always wished was mine. I could never compete with you, so I didn't even try. To be honest, I forgot about you until one night you came back to haunt me with a vengeance."

Jack looks confused. "What are you talking about?"

I catch Kim's eye and she looks absolutely horrified and my heart goes out to her. It can't be nice discovering your husband was a bully, and she appears shaken. However, my attention is dragged back to the conversation as Ben looks across at me and shakes his head, looking so worried I wonder what on earth he's going to say.

"I was heading home late one night after finishing work at a bar in Brighton and something captured my attention. I heard a noise coming from an alley and as I peered in, the light from the door opening caused me to look and I recognised you immediately. I saw you with a girl, she appeared drunk and you were holding her up. I made to go and help, but the door shut and everything went dark. I heard you laughing though. As I moved closer, I saw you pressed up against her and the sounds you were making told me I shouldn't interfere. Obviously, you were doing something you wouldn't thank me for interrupting and so I moved away. But something about it didn't sit well with me. It wasn't right, and I suppose a warning siren went off in my head. It was all a little one-sided. The sounds were coming from you alone and so I went back and then I saw her, slumped on the ground. You had left, and she was lying there, out cold and cast aside like a used piece of trash."

I think my life flashes before me at this moment and I can't do anything but stare as if I'm a spectator watching my own life crash and burn.

Jack shouts, "You're a fucking lunatic, you're making this up."

He looks at Kim and says angrily, "The guy's a madman. That never happened. Why would I rape someone? You heard him, I was popular for Christ's sake, women were all over me. Why would I take an unwilling one?"

Suddenly, the screen behind Ben flickers and Ben sneers, "I thought you might say that, well, why don't you watch a little video we put together for promotional purposes."

As we stare at the screen, I hear a gasp from across the room as Evelyn cries out, "Oh my god."

CHAPTER 40

EVELYN

I'm not sure what's happening here, but my life is unravelling fast. Charles has been moody, irritable and downright rude ever since he returned from the morning spent on the boat and I can tell he's been drinking. Now this speech is changing everything as Emma's boyfriend delivers blow upon blow to the surrounding guests, and as I stare at the screen, I can actually hear my heart thumping.

The image is of me, walking past the gym and I know immediately when this was - the night I am trying so hard to forget. I'm on my own and looking around as if I'm waiting for someone and I look across at Jack who is standing like a statue.

I see a man walking up behind me in the video and from the back it looks like Jack. But he wasn't there; he told me it wasn't him.

My breath hitches as I watch him wrap his hand around my face and cover my mouth and drag me into the cupboard. As the door slams, the tears fall fast down my face as I remember exactly what was going on in there. I can feel a few concerned looks thrown my way as the crowd starts to

194

shift awkwardly on their feet and Charles hisses, "What the hell is going on, Evelyn, is that…"

The tape must fast forward because the door opens and the camera pans in on Jack heading out of the cupboard, zipping up his pants and smirking cockily, and there's a hushed gasp of horror as just about everyone looks at him and then me.

I hear a shocked, "Oh my god, Jack." and recognise Kim's voice as she starts to sob and then as the door opens, I cringe when I see myself head outside, looking up and down the hallway before I straighten my clothing and walk away. However, it's obvious I'm more than happy about what happened and Charles hisses, "I think you have some explaining to do."

The screen changes and I close my eyes as the images from the lift play out of when I first met Jack. The gasp of horror reveals that the audience is watching every moment of a sordid encounter showing us at our worst. I remember it all so vividly because I was like an animal myself and I feel the shame wash over me as Jack shouts, "Turn it off, this is an invasion of privacy. So what if we had fun? I never forced her; you can see how much she loves it."

I stand shaking as the tears run down my face and take a step back as Charles grips my arm hard and anchors me beside him, hissing angrily, "You will stay and face up to what you've done, you fucking whore."

It feels as if I am now the most hated person on the planet as I feel the hostile looks thrown my way and then Ben says loudly, "You can see what sort of man Jack Parker is and he obviously never grew out of his desire to take women by force. So, Jack, how does it feel to be named and shamed? Mentally beaten and hated by everyone. Standing there exposed while a bigger bully brings you down and there is absolutely nothing you can do about it and you will have to live with the shameful memory forever. Welcome to my world, Jack because you are about to discover what it's like to feel real fear because I'm guessing there are two men in this room who have quite the grudge against you, so I would start running if I were you."

Charles drops my arm and moves away, and he doesn't move alone. Suddenly, I hear Chloe shout with real fear in her voice, "JOHN, NO!"

It appears as if all hell breaks loose as we hear a roar, "You fucking bastard, I'm going to kill you."

I gasp when I see John launch himself at Jack and Charles soon joins in and the sound of screaming ricochets around the room as the place erupts into violence.

The next thing I know, I see Kim standing before me looking utterly heartbroken and then she shocks the hell out of me by saying sadly, "Are you ok, Evelyn?"

I blink in surprise as I stare at a woman who is mentally ruined, shaking with emotion with the tears running down her face.

"But…"

I am fully waiting for her to strike me, punch me, cause me physical pain to replace the mental one she is obviously going through, but she just looks so destroyed, it's as if she has no strength left for the fight. Then she shakes her head sadly and slips her hand in mine, and as chaos breaks out all around us, she pulls me from the room.

THE NIGHT AIR feels like antiseptic on a burn as she walks purposefully towards the beach, pulling me along behind her. I am so shocked I can't even protest as she steers us away from the madness Ben's words have created.

The noise soon fades into the background and an eerie

silence descends on us as she says in a dull voice, "I'm so sorry, Evelyn."

From somewhere, I find my voice and say in a whisper, "Why, you've done nothing to apologise for, it's me who should apologise to you?"

"For what, being taken in by my husband? I kind of understand how that can happen, so how can I blame you for his actions?"

"But I was to blame just as much as him. I'm so sorry, Kim, I never meant to hurt you, but I was blinded by my attraction to him."

"I know what that feels like."

She pulls me down to sit on the sand next to her and wraps her arms around her knees, drawing them close as if to protect her from the harsh reality.

"You see, finding out my husband is a sex predator is not the worst moment of my life."

"It's not."

She shakes her head sadly. "To be honest, nothing surprises me anymore about that man. The worst thing I heard tonight was before it all kicked off."

"What did you hear?"

I can't believe that anything could be worse than what we just went through and she sobs, "Jack knew I always wanted children. He knew it was a huge part of me and yet he never told me that he couldn't have them, not until we came here. I always thought he had a problem because I got myself checked out when we failed to get pregnant. At first, I was compassionate and felt sorry for him but he was so angry and dismissive and that's why we argued. I'm not surprised he came after you, that's typical Jack. He likes to be in control and he was losing it with me. He pushed me away because he didn't like the conversation I wanted to have. It's obvious he never wanted children at all because

Chloe told me he discussed his vasectomy operation with John."

Reaching out, I place my arm around her shoulders and it strikes me how messed up this is. She should hate me, be shouting at me, yet she is opening up a part of her soul that makes me feel even worse about what I've done.

Her soft cries are the only sound as she lets the tears fall for a future she wanted above everything. Then she takes a deep breath and whispers, "What will happen now, I'm guessing your husband will be angry."

Thinking of Charles leaves me cold inside. Empty, as if he no longer has any meaning in my life, and I sigh. "His pride will be wounded, but knowing him he'll brush it aside and use it to keep me in line."

"That's horrible."

"He's a horrible man. It appears we have that in common at least. We married extremely nasty men."

"What do you think is happening right now?"

"With any luck, John will kill them both and do us the favour of not having to face them again."

Kim laughs softly. "Here's hoping."

"You know Kim…" I have to voice the words that can't stay unspoken much longer and I sigh heavily.

"I am so sorry. I've done something I'm not proud of and I was blind to your feelings and thought it wouldn't hurt just this once. I was so wrapped up in what I wanted, I never once stopped to think about the damage it would do to you, and I will never forgive myself for that."

"Thank you."

I stare out at the black sea that ripples in the moonlight and say sadly, "What will you do now?"

"Divorce him, move out, start again somewhere new. I still have my job so I'll maybe rent somewhere, lick my wounds and hope that my future isn't as brutal as my past. How about you?"

"The same, I guess, although I'll have to find a job and fast. It just shows how stupid I've been because even though it looks as if I have everything, in reality I have nothing. No personal wealth, no possessions, even the house is in Charles's name. It's likely I'll end up having to move in with my parents. That will be a difficult conversation."

Kim sounds concerned. "You will be entitled to half of his money, surely."

"Maybe, but knowing Charles, he will fight me every step of the way. It's fine though, I can't be unhappy anymore. You know, as bad as this sounds, I'm glad that happened. I'm ashamed of what I did and always will be, but it has forced change that was long overdue. Maybe Ben has done us both a favour, although I'm not so sure about Chloe."

"Do you think that woman was her, I couldn't tell?"

Thinking of the look on Chloe's face and John's reaction, I nod. "I think it must have been. I saw her face when she saw the images on the screen. She looked horrified, destroyed even, and John looked so angry I knew it could only be personal."

"Yes, I saw Ben watching her carefully. Do you think he knew it was her and brought her here to confront the man who..."

She breaks off and I reach for her hand and squeeze it gently. "I'm guessing we were all brought here for a reason and this was no coincidence. Maybe there's more to come; I don't know if I can cope if there is."

Kim squeezes my hand and sighs. "It can't be worse than what just happened? It's weird how something so terrible can happen in a place that is so stunning it takes my breath away. It doesn't seem right somehow. It's the ugly side of beauty, much like my husband's behaviour, really. He may be beautiful on the outside but is ugly inside. It appears that looks count for nothing in the long term because who would want to be with a man like that?"

We are in no hurry to return to a place where our problems are waiting to determine what happens next. Instead, we sit staring out to sea as if all the answers lie there. A strange feeling of calm settles over me as I sit beside a woman who is far richer than me where it counts. Kim, unlike her husband, is beautiful inside and out and I know she will be just fine – me, I'm not so sure.

CHAPTER 41

EMMA

*W*hat is happening? The place is in chaos, and I don't know where to look first. The men are all fighting and weirdly the staff are just watching as if they've paid for a ticket. I can see Chloe shaking and instinctively rush over and take her arm, "Come on, babe, let's get out of here."

To my surprise, she doesn't argue despite the fact her partner is knocking pieces out of Jack. Not that I blame him after what I just saw, and I can't quite believe it happened at all.

We head out to the quiet reception and to my surprise Ben follows us.

"Chloe." His voice is deep and apologetic and she stills beside me.

"Chloe, please, let me explain."

I look between them in confusion as Chloe starts to sob, angrily brushing the tears away as Ben says softly, "Come, I'll explain everything."

"Maybe it's best if I come too."

I stare at Ben pointedly and he nods and we follow him to

a room behind the reception desk. As soon as the door closes, it silences the noise coming from the bar. A welcome calm descends on the place and we just wait for Ben to speak.

He sits opposite Chloe and I take a seat to the side and he says softly, "I'm so sorry, Chloe, that must have come as quite a shock."

"Just a bit." Chloe looks so shaken I wonder if I should get her a cup of tea, or a brandy, but I don't want to leave her. She looks so devastated and Ben sighs heavily. "I changed my mind a thousand times about bringing you here, revealing your attacker's identity and putting you through yet more pain when the last thing you probably want is to remember."

Chloe nods, "Then why do it and how did you even know where I was?"

Ben shakes his head and I'm surprised to see a little of his cool manner desert him.

"Maybe I should start at the beginning. It may answer a few of your questions."

He looks up and as our eyes meet, he says with a smile. "Let me order some drinks to settle our nerves and then I'll begin."

He lifts the receiver and speaks firmly into it, ordering three brandies with coffees.

Then he looks at Chloe and I see him battling with something and I think I hold my breath as I wait for yet another secret to come out.

"You heard me talk of my childhood. It wasn't the easiest of beginnings but all that changed when I was adopted. I finally had the parents I always longed for and quite frankly, they saved me. But those early years linger in your memory like unhealed wounds. I suppose I was always an outsider, always on the edge of the group, never included in things and always chosen last. I came to expect it. Nothing ever changed, even when my clothes were smarter, newer and my hair washed and styled. I was always the misfit and bullies like to prey on people like me to make themselves look good."

He looks up and as our eyes meet, I feel a prickling sensation deep inside. Something's wrong about this, I'm not sure why, but there's a sense of something coming that I'm not going to like.

"Jack bullied me for my entire school life. He beat me, taunted me, and ridiculed me. Always set me up for a fall and he was the monster under my bed and my hatred of him was the skeleton in my closet. I suppose as time went by the wound deepened and began to fester. It turned out I was good at something though; I had a knack for facts and figures that only grew the more interested I became. Despite my start and Jack's best efforts, I did well at school and when I left, I vowed to make him pay one day because men like that should never get away with ruining another person's life."

We are interrupted by a brief knock at the door and a waitress heads inside carrying a tray which she sets down on the desk.

Ben smiles his thanks and waits for her to leave before offering us both a mug of coffee, before taking one himself.

He carries on. "To be honest, I forgot about him while I attended college. During that time, I worked two jobs and invested the money in stocks and shares. I was good - more than good, and my money doubled, then trebled and hasn't stopped since. The night I saw Jack in the alley, everything came rushing back. The hurt, the pain, the hatred and the desire for revenge. Perhaps that was what brought me back to find you, knowing the sort of child he was and the man he obviously became."

Chloe sobs. "Why didn't you report him? I was made out to be at fault. They blamed me at first until they found the drug in my system."

"Oh my god, Chloe, no, that's terrible."

Reaching out, I stroke her back and try to offer the only comfort I can and she shrugs. "It was a long time ago; it took a while, but I moved on. Like Ben said though, it left its scars, and it was only when we came here and I had a disturbing altercation with your father, that I finally told John everything."

"My father." Ben looks shocked and Chloe sighs. "In town, he gave me his room key and told me to use it. He said it was obvious I was lusting after him, well obviously that was a lie and a figment of his imagination but I'm glad he's gone. I'm sorry for you, Ben. That was devastating to watch."

Shaking his head, Ben shrugs. "I was looking forward to it, it's why I couldn't wait any longer to bring this all out in the open. Why should I continue to pay for scum like that to enjoy my hospitality? He had seen enough, and I had my sweet revenge."

Once again, he looks at me and something in his eyes stirs a memory deep inside. I can't quite place it though, and I can tell he knows because he turns back to Chloe.

"Facebook was all I needed to keep track of him. I hate to admit, but I'm pretty techy and soon found a way to duplicate accounts and be included on friend's lists. I always intended to make him pay for what he did to you, but at the time I couldn't get involved. I mean, who would believe it wasn't me who drugged and well…"

I look at him sharply because maybe that's exactly what happened, and he's framing Jack. However, deep in my heart I know that's not the case. Ben is a good man; I just know he is because the compassion in his eyes just can't be fabricated.

"I checked and there was no CCTV in the alley. No evidence to link Jack with you, and so I bided my time. I found out your name; it wasn't difficult, just a word in the right ear, and then I added you on Facebook. I watched you over the years, the pictures of your friends, family, how you progressed and was just glad you seemed happy and had moved on with your life."

"But I still don't understand why you brought me here to face something so horrific with no warning."

"Because I know only too well what trauma does to a person. It's probably affected your life, shaped you and made you fear the very thing that brought you down. Nobody ever recovers from those jagged memories that cut you when you least expect it. I'm guessing you know that already, so I brought you here for closure. To cleanse the past and start afresh. I suppose I wanted to apologise, to help you in any way I can, maybe I felt guilty for not stepping up when I had the chance, back you up and tell your side of the story. The trouble is, I was still a kid myself who had a bad record with standing up to bullies, and Jack Parker was a huge black cloud from my past that affected me in my present."

I see a steely gleam in his eye as he says firmly, "Not now though, the cards have shuffled and now I'm in a position to right those wrongs and help put something right that should never have taken this long."

Suddenly, the door flies open and I stare in shock as John bursts in looking frantic and as soon as he sees Chloe, he races across and pulls her into his arms, stroking her hair and kissing her over and over again. He looks awful, as if he fought a war, with his knuckles torn and bleeding and dark angry bruises on his arms and neck that look painful.

He pulls back and my breath hitches when I see the love shining from Chloe's eyes as she whispers, "It's over, John."

He runs his thumb across her cheeks, wiping her tears away, and nods. "Yes, no more secrets."

Ben sits back and watches the scene, and I see a thousand emotions pass across his face.

Chloe looks at him and smiles. "Thank you. I'm still not

sure if I should be thanking you, but I know you brought us here with all the best intentions. What happens now?"

He smiles. "You carry on enjoying your holiday at my expense and I get rid of the unwelcome visitors. Any time you need to talk, I am here for you and I hope, like me, you can take closure from this and go on and live your best life without the past clouding your sky."

John looks confused and Chloe smiles. "I think I can."

She looks over at me and says gratefully, "Thanks, Emma, you've got a good one there. I'd hold on to him if I were you."

I watch as John takes her hand and leads her gently away and as the door slams, it's as if it dislodges the memory from its hiding place in my mind and a cold feeling creeps over me as I turn and face the man I remember from my past.

Now I know who he is.

CHAPTER 42

KIM

*E*velyn and I finally make it back to the resort, and I'm not sure what's going to happen next. We wait for the lift and I look at her with concern.

"Will you be ok?"

"I expect so, will you?"

"I know so."

I smile and she looks so apologetic I shake my head. "What happened with Jack was something you couldn't control. It's obvious he's a master manipulator, and I should know that more than anyone."

She says sadly, "I don't know how you can forgive me."

"We're all victims, Evelyn, but not anymore. Never again, promise me that at least."

"I will." She still looks troubled, and I know something is preying on her mind as I see the fresh tears build.

"What is it?"

"I just don't understand. You see, Jack arranged to meet at the gym that night for exactly what happened. The whole time we were, um, together, I never saw his face. It was so dark and he stayed behind me for most of it. I thought it was him, why wouldn't it be, but the next day he told me he loved you and didn't want anything to happen between us? I was angry because it already had, and when I told him as much, he looked confused and told me we had only kissed in the lift. He made out it was someone else and ever since I have been imagining all sorts. I thought I'd been attacked, and it's been a hard thing to deal with."

"But it was him all the time." I finish her sentence and feel even more disgusted with my husband than I was before. "Typical Jack, really. He says one thing and does another. I think he has a split personality. He's been like that for most of our married life. He does things he regrets and then pretends they never happened and always tries to shift the blame to make himself look good. It took me a while to realise that and this is a classic example of it."

"Why is he so cruel?"

"You saw him, you heard what Ben said; he's damaged, and probably needs a good counsellor to sort his head out. Well, that's *his* problem because I'm done with him. Forever."

"You're so strong." Evelyn looks wistful and I shake my head. "Not really, just at the end of the line. Anyway, will you be ok?"

The lift stops at her floor and she smiles with a bravery I doubt she feels inside. "I'll be fine, Charles won't say anything, not when everyone saw what happened. He wouldn't dare. He hates drawing attention to himself in a bad way because he's all about appearances and wants to be admired, not detested."

I step out and smile reassuringly. "You know where I am, good luck, Evelyn."

"You too, Kim."

As the doors close, I walk slowly along the hallway, suddenly scared of what I may find. The man on that screen, the man Ben described, is a monster.

I married a monster.

Picturing the husband I loved so much I forgave him anything, makes my heart weep. What happened to him, has he always been so damaged? Thinking back on Ben's childhood, I know my answer. Things will never be right with him; he needs professional help, but I no longer care enough to stick around to make sure he gets it.

My heart thumps as I reach our room, and I tentatively open the door and step inside. The room is in semi-darkness, lit only by the moon, and I see a shadowy figure sitting in the chair in front of the window, with his head in his hands.

"Jack." My voice is soft, testing his mood, and he raises his eyes to mine and sounds so broken as he whispers, "I'm sorry, Kim."

"I know."

I expected that, it's nothing new because he always is – sorry that is. I've lost count of how many times I've heard those words over the years and I know that's all they are – words.

"Do you need a doctor?" My voice is hard and practical, and he winces a little as he touches his fingers to his face. "Probably, but I'll live."

Stepping a little closer, I see the results of a severe beating. Even in the darkness I can make out the damage inflicted on his once perfect face and he winces as he holds his body telling me he is in a lot of pain.

"We should clean you up."

"It's fine, just surface damage, I'll be ok."

"Are you sure about that?"

"Yes, of course. Despite was you saw, I never attacked Evelyn. It was a moment of madness after our encounter in the lift earlier. She made it obvious she was up for it, and I thought she liked the excitement. Did she look as if she

209

objected – no? If I'm guilty of anything, it's screwing around behind your back, which hurts me the most."

"Why? You don't really care what I think because if you did, you wouldn't have kept on doing it all these years. You see, Jack, Evelyn isn't the first and won't be the last and if you think that's where our problem lies then I'm worried for your sanity."

"Then what is the problem?"

"Chloe."

"That wasn't me. You only have a fucked-up version from a man who hates me. He's deluded and making something up that never happened – with me."

"I believe him."

Jack's eyes flash as he snarls, "Above me, you'd believe a man you don't even know above your own husband. Who's fucked-up now?"

"If it wasn't you, which I doubt, it doesn't matter anyway. Like the man said, Karma's a bitch, and you just got everything you deserved. Why should I care when my own husband lied to me?"

"About what? I've told you what happened with Evelyn, it's the truth."

"I'm not talking about Evelyn!" I start to yell because this man infuriates me so much. Even now he is trying damage limitation and it's frustrating the hell out of me.

"This is about *us*, Jack, it's about the fact you lied to me about the most important thing – children."

"What are you talking about, I never lied to you, I never promised you children? For god's sake, Kim, you're seriously raising this issue again. I told you I can't have them, get over it."

I don't know how I keep my voice calm as I say firmly, "There's a difference between not being *able* to have them and *choosing* not to have them. Maybe the fact you've had an operation to take away that chance has something to do with it."

"What are you talking about?"

"Your vasectomy, you idiot, the very operation that takes away a man's ability to have children, at least yours wasn't as traumatic an experience as John's was. Lucky you."

The bitterness sits between us like an impenetrable wall because I am so done with this man. Whatever he says next won't change a thing because I won't believe a word of it.

He shakes his head and says gruffly, "So, once again you believe a stranger over your own husband. Way to go Kim, ten out of ten for loyalty. Now which one of us is fucked-up?"

"What does it matter anyway, Jack. I think we both know this marriage is over, and tonight was just the match that lit the fuse. If I'm honest, it's been over for some time, so maybe it's a good thing we never had children because I'm not sure I would want them to have a father like you, anyway."

"So, that's it, you're ending our marriage because I won't give you children, so much for love, it turns out you're not worth much yourself."

"Think what you like, I no longer care. You know, Jack, we could have had it all. Even if tonight never happened, it was inevitable. We aren't meant to be together, and that's been obvious for some time. Maybe this has done us a favour and we can move on and be happier. I know I will be because for all the happiness you gave me, it was buried under the pain, humiliation and psychological trauma you heaped on top of it. Anyway, I've said what I came here to say, I'll let you sort your shit out on your own and see if they've got another room. I'll collect my stuff in the morning."

"You're leaving me – now?"

Jack sounds incredulous, which doesn't surprise me. I almost know what he's going to say next and if he's anything it's predictable as his mood switches. "Please don't leave me, Kim, I love you, we can work this out. I need you."

"I can't deal with this tonight, Jack, we'll talk in the morning."

I make to leave and he groans as he shifts from the chair and hisses, "Help me, Kim, I'm in so much pain. I need you."

"To patch you up. No, you don't need me, Jack, you need professional help and I'm not qualified. Just let me have my space."

"I can't let you walk away; I need you with me."

"That's not your decision to make, it's mine and I can't deal with any more tonight. I'll see you tomorrow, try to get some sleep."

As I walk away from Jack, it feels surprisingly good and I'm amazed to discover that this hasn't broken me. It's given me the courage I needed to make a decision that's been brewing for some time. I am walking away from him, my marriage and my old life. I'm walking away with my head held high and the determination to do what's right – for me.

Strangely, as I walk down the carpeted hallway to freedom, I do so with a smile on my face because it's as if a huge burden has shifted. I'm free - of him. I know that whatever he says won't change that and if anything, even if it was all fabricated, I no longer care because this is my one-way ticket out of a marriage that should have ended years ago.

CHAPTER 43

EVELYN

A strange sense of calm accompanies me to my room, which surprises me a little. After the evening I've had I should be in bits, worried, fearful and ashamed. Thinking of Charles's reaction no longer worries me. Whatever he says or does can't be any worse than what I've done to myself, and it ends now. Seeing Kim, so strong, so kind and so compassionate makes me want to be a better version of myself.

It's over.

The life I thought was a dream is finally over and even if I do end up moving back to live with my parents, at least I'll be free. Start again, find a job and learn that nothing in life is free for a reason. It's up to the individual to take charge of their life for more than just money. For self-worth, for happiness and fulfilment. Some women get that through raising a family, they define themselves through that. I'm not in any position to take charge of another life when I have made such a bad job of my own.

It's with a twinge of fear inside that I let myself into the room and hear Charles moving around in the bathroom.

He must hear the door because he heads out and my face must fall when I see the evidence of the fight staining his face.

"You've got a bloody nerve coming back here."

He stares at me angrily and I say regretfully, "I'm sorry, Charles."

"So you should be. What I saw on that screen will live with me to my dying day; the moment I discovered my wife was a whore."

I let him speak because by the looks of him he's so worked up, any words I utter would fall on deaf ears. He grinds out angrily, "How do you think that made me look? The man whose wife couldn't wait to fuck a stranger in a cupboard. I felt the pity in the room – for me."

He looks incredibly angry and I can almost taste it as he spits, "I'm so done with you. Trying to give you everything you want; working all hours just to buy you things, make you happy and for what?"

"I never asked you to, I begged you to let me get a job."

"STOP TALKING!"

His voice is so loud it's almost a scream and I stare at him in horror as he loses it completely. He shouts, "Everything I have done was for you. Every thought in my head was for our future, to make *you* happy and to be rich and successful. I wanted you to be proud to call me your husband and make you the envy of all your friends, and for what? A woman who has nothing interesting to say and is shit in bed."

"You made me this way."

It's my turn to scream now. All the years of pent-up frustration bubble over and I shout, "I never asked for this. I just wanted a loving husband who didn't stifle me, suffocate me, and make me feel worthless. I was just your barbie doll to dress up and play with when you had the time. You are so boring Charles, I want to scream. I never wanted your possessions or your money, I just wanted you. Not anymore, though. Not now, I want more and that doesn't involve money. I want to feel free, happy and look forward to the future, instead of dreading waking up the next day. What I'm saying is, Charles, I want a divorce."

To my surprise, he starts to laugh, but there's not a trace of humour in it.

"So, this is what it's all about. You think you'll walk away with half my hard-earned money and set yourself up, no doubt with a new lover every week. Well, darling, reality check, there is no money."

Taking a deep breath, I try to maintain an even tone and calm this situation down. "Do you really think this all about money, haven't you listened to a word I just said?"

I look at him in surprise because it's as if he hasn't listened at all.

Instead, he just snarls, "I can't deal with this now, there's more important business to attend to."

"More important than our marriage. That just about sums it all up."

I break off and say sadly, "It was always more about the business and even now, it still is."

"Yes, it's all about the business because that's the machine that feeds us, gives us nice things and expensive houses, cars and holidays. Those jewels you wear, the designer clothes you drip in, are all paid for out of the business. So, let me tell you one more time, the business will *always* be more important than you and now, as I said, I don't have time to deal with you and your tantrum. I need to go and find out if I still have a business after the text I received yesterday."

"What are you talking about?"

For the first time since I met Charles, I see real fear in his eyes. A real sense of foreboding that takes priority now because its obvious something extremely bad has happened, judging by the wild look in his eye and the desperation on his face. I'm not stupid enough to think it's there because of me. Something is badly wrong with his business and Charles appears to be falling without a safety net.

He glares at me before grabbing his briefcase and storming out of the room, leaving me watching him go with a strange mixture of relief and worry.

I've never seen him so crazy. He almost looks unhinged and yet it's not because of what I did, something is very wrong with the business side of things and if it does bring him down, I'm not sure how he'll cope with that.

As I sit on the bed and place my head in my hands, I let it all out. The feelings that I have kept hidden for so long, the shattered dreams and broken promises, all merge with the self-loathing that I have felt for some time now. Hatred of Charles and my situation are the bricks around my neck that make me sink to rock bottom, and I cry for the girl I was and the woman I became. Whatever happens next is immaterial because there's no going back now. If we lose it all, it's fine because there is nothing worth keeping, anyway.

CHAPTER 44

The penny drops like a bomb and I look at Ben with a mixture of interest and disbelief. "I know you."

He nods. "I wondered when you'd remember."

"It was so long ago; it certainly feels that way. I can't believe it's you, you're so different, more..."

I struggle for words because he is so different. Everything about him is different and he laughs softly. "I'm no longer that shy, slightly nerdy guy who idolised you at college. The kid fresh out of school who thought girls like you were princesses. I put you on a pedestal and worshipped the ground you walked on. I would have done anything for you until you threw it all back in my face."

"We were never together, never friends, what are you talking about?" I stare at him in surprise because yes, I knew Benjamin Wheeler but he was never high enough on my radar to warrant a second look. Admittedly he helped me out with course work on occasion but we never met socially, unless you count the time he asked me out but I thought he knew I was never interested. Now things are different, so maybe he brought me here to persuade me to stay because he's held a torch for me all these years.

If anything, I feel flattered and smile smugly. "You went to a lot of trouble to get me here – us here, how did you manage it, it's impressive?"

He swirls the brandy around his glass and looks at me with a hint of a smile. "I told you, I'm quite techy and Facebook enabled me to run an ad that only went to the people I wanted it to. There was no competition, no testing of the facilities. I just wanted to bring my past to my present to set me free into my future."

He must sense my confusion because he laughs. "Let me explain. You see I wasn't joking when I said that Buddhism interested me. It was the principles that I identified with more than anything. The harder I studied, the more I believed in Karma. It is a term about the cycle of cause and effect. According to the theory of Karma, what happens to a person, happens because they caused it with their actions. Things that happen in the past decides your fate in the future. Cause and effect. As you sow, so shall you reap. Are you still with me?"

I must look confused because he raises his eyes. "Then let me spell it out for you. To receive happiness, peace, love, and friendship, one must BE happy, peaceful, loving, and a true friend. Whatever a person puts out into the universe will come back to them. I was so wrapped up in bitterness I was denying myself something that would ultimately make me happy, so that's why I brought you all here. A cleansing of the past, to bring me happiness in the future."

I smile because I'm guessing why he brought me here. To seduce me, the girl he could never have, the woman he thought about ever since and wanted so badly he engineered this whole thing to win her heart. I smile with encouragement and whisper, "So, now you have me here, what are you planning? I mean, it's come as quite a shock, a nice one though, but what is this bright future you are planning and how does it affect me?"

"It doesn't."

"Excuse me."

He laughs but I can't see the joke and he leans back in his chair and I watch in fascination as his eyes sparkle with an energy that captivates me.

"The thing is, Emma, one must accept something in order to change it. If all one sees is an enemy, or a negative character trait, then they are not and cannot be focused on a higher level of existence. I gave you that chance. To see if you had become a better person, learned from the past and weren't the manipulative bitch I remembered."

"What are you saying?" I stare at him in confusion because this isn't the way I thought this conversation was going to go. He sounds almost angry as he laughs bitterly, "I can't believe you don't remember how you belittled me, humiliated me and made me feel like a piece of dirt you trod in."

I am wracking my brains to remember what I did that was so bad and he leans forward and snarls, "Then let me enlighten you. When you dropped me a note on my desk, I was curious. Why would you give me anything when you hardly knew I existed? I was ecstatic when I saw the handwritten note asking me to meet you at the pizza restaurant that evening. You told me you were interested and had been for some time, that you wanted to get to know me and like a fool I believed every word."

I almost can't look him in the eye as I remember back to a time I was off the rails and a little wild. It was something we did back then, little dares to make our days interesting. To cheer ourselves up and make a day seem worthwhile. Yes, I was popular and yes, I had my pick of the most popular guys, which is why my friends dared me to trap a geeky guy who would do anything I asked and I chose Benjamin Wheeler. He was so wet behind the ears and wore the most disgusting glasses. His clothes were old fashioned and his hair lacked any sort of modern style. He looked like an old man in a young man's body and we thought it would be funny to watch.

I feel confused as to how it affected him this much and he laughs out loud.

"Still the same I see. Now you know what I'm talking about and you still can't see anything wrong with what you did. Well, I sat in that Pizza restaurant for two hours with your friends at the next table, giggling and staring at me the entire time. I couldn't understand it and it's only now I realise they were probably texting you and sending you photos of the fool you stood up. I was so sure it was a mistake. Something had happened to you and I was worried - can you believe I was actually worried that you'd had an accident, or were hurt?"

He looks so angry and I feel a little alarmed as he growls, "The next day you cornered me in the hallway and apologised. You told me something had come up at home and you wanted to make it up to me and to meet you after school by the south entrance. Like a fool, I did as you asked, desperate to believe that you actually wanted me. I waited for one hour that time and yes, you did show up in the end but you weren't alone. You made out with one of the guys from the football team right in front of me and then laughed in my face. You whispered something in his ear and he glared at me and told me to stop perving on his girl and called me a piece of shit for watching women. He came over and pushed me to the ground and kicked me hard in the ribs, while you laughed as if it was a huge joke. Then he warned me to stay away because if he saw me near any girl again, he would come and find me with the rest of the team. Do you know how hard that was for me? Now you know about my childhood, the bullying in school and the struggle I had getting to where I was? It all came back to haunt me that day. The pain, the loneliness the sense of never belonging, having no friends and being worthless. You made me feel like that because you were a cruel bitch who thought it was a laugh. Well, Karma's a bitch as they say because that's all you were to me."

"What are you saying?" He seems so angry, unreasonably so in my mind because who holds a grudge against something kids do all these years later?

"Let's be clear. I brought you here to see what I became. The boy you wrote off as not worth anything. I wanted to see if you remembered me and felt sorry for how you treated me. But all you saw was my wealth, my fine clothes and expensive toys. You saw a meal ticket and a life of luxury that you wouldn't have to lift a finger to create. You wanted a trophy on your arm and a man your friends would envy. Well, I never wanted you. I just wanted closure on a past that still haunts me now. Now I've seen how you ended up, it's no surprise you have a failed business, probably because in order to make something a success you actually have to work at it, and hard. No relationship to speak of, probably because you're not really the sort of woman men see as the marrying kind. So, how does it feel knowing that you learned nothing worth shit for existing in a grown-up world? Now, if you'll excuse me, I have an empire to run and you can see yourself out because you have some packing to do."

"But…" My head is spinning as his words sink in. He doesn't want me; it was revenge and nothing more. But he's turned out so gorgeous, successful and desirable, there must be something I can do to repair the damage. Mustering every emotion I own, I let the tears flow and sob, "I'm so sorry,

Ben. You have every right to hate me, hell, I hate myself for what I did to you. I never meant to hurt you, please believe me, let me make it up to you, please, give me that chance."

He stares at me in surprise. "You're really doing this, asking me for a second chance but why?"

"Because meeting you again made me realise how much I liked you - like you now. It's not about your life and how well you've done, it's about how much I enjoyed spending time with you, stirring a pot that had been left to boil dry. Please give me the chance to make it up to you, give me a week, two perhaps. I can prove that I've changed and I'm not that woman you spoke of back in the past. I am a better person now and surely everyone deserves a second chance at least."

I'm almost hopeful as he looks a little unsure and stares at me with a sad expression. Then he shakes his head and says bitterly, "When you look at me, Emma, you see the wealthy entrepreneur and the successful man I became. You gave me a chance because you were swayed by the gifts, the attention and the packaging. You were blinded by what I could give you and never realised it's a two-way street. I want a woman who sees beyond all this. Sees the boy I was and the man I am now. Not the businessman, the person behind the suit. That's not you Emma and it never will be. Anyway, you need to leave because at 8am a cab is arriving to take you to the airport where I have booked you on the first flight out of here. Maybe you will think of how you treat people from now on because everyone has feelings, no matter how much money, how many friends, or how little they've got. They are all people like you and deserve respect and acceptance, regardless of their situation in life. Look on this as my parting gift. Work on your attitude and maybe you will be successful one day, both in business and in love."

I can't even look at the man, how dare he preach to me as if he's above me? I am fine as I am; I have my own business for goodness's sake. Just because he has all this, he thinks he can talk down to me, reject me as something worthless under his shoe and manipulate me for his own pleasure just so he can feel good about one little thing that happened years ago.

A sudden feeling touches me inside, and now I know how it feels to be the underdog. I don't like it one bit, so I turn my back on him and walk away. As I leave, I bump into someone and as he pushes past me, I see a look of fury on Evelyn's husband's face. Something in his eye tells me he's unhinged and briefly I wonder what that means for Ben.

As I walk away, I find myself smiling. Yes, Ben, Karma certainly is a bitch.

CHAPTER 45

EVELYN

*W*hen I wake the next morning, it takes a moment to remember the events of yesterday, but they soon come flooding back in all their horrific glory. I blink as the morning sun hits me square in the eye and the soft breeze wafts through the double doors that lead to the balcony.

Suddenly, I hear a terse, "It's about time you woke up, we don't have long, get dressed."

I make out Charles sitting in the chair by the open door and by the looks of it, he's been there all night. His eyes are bloodshot and his face bruised and scratched, a chilling reminder of what happens when a man loses control.

He's dressed in a smart short-sleeved shirt and chinos and his hair is still wet from the shower.

"What time is it?"

"7.30, we have a breakfast meeting at 8."

"What breakfast meeting, who with?"

"Ben."

"What's it about?"

"Business."

His words are short and laced with underlying tension, and I know better than to question him further. I can tell he's on edge, and I'm just grateful he's not still talking about what happened yesterday. Maybe we can be civil for the rest of the trip and somehow make it home unscathed, where I know things will have to change. I can't live like this anymore; I can't live with *him* anymore and so I nod and just head to the bathroom to make myself look as presentable as I can for the mysterious meeting with the elusive Mr Wheeler.

Deciding on a maxi dress and white strappy sandals, I pull my hair into a sleek ponytail and hide behind the largest pair of sunglasses I own. I'm a little surprised I've been included in this meeting at all because Charles doesn't like to mix business with his personal life.

We hardly say two words to each other as we walk through reception and if I notice anything, it's how eerie it feels here after the events of the night before.

To my surprise, the waiter doesn't show us to our usual table on the edge of the terrace overlooking the ocean but says reverently, "Mr Wheeler has requested your company in his suite."

My heart sinks as Charles gets that pompous look on his face that he wears so well when he thinks he's better than everyone else, and we follow the waiter to an elevator that lies at the side of the room.

We head inside and the waiter presses the button for the top floor and smiles. "Mr Wheeler will greet you. This lift heads straight to his penthouse. Enjoy your breakfast."

He looks down and as the door closes Charles says tersely, "He had better have a good explanation for all of this."

"Explanation for what, what's happened?"

Charles growls, "What's happened, *darling*..." He sounds sarcastic as he emphasises the last word. "We may have just lost everything because of that man, so shut up and let me do the talking."

Charles taps his foot impatiently, and it surprises me that his words don't mean a thing to me. We may have lost everything he says, I already know we have.

The door opens straight into a luxurious apartment with a panoramic view of the sea. It actually takes my breath away because where ours is impressive, this one is magnificent. Soft white settees are positioned in the centre of the room facing the sea, and deep pile rugs are scattered at intervals over the marble floors. Exquisite furniture is strategically placed around the room and fresh bouquets of Ben's favourite lotus flower scent the room with an intoxicating aroma. There's a sense of tranquillity and peace in this room that calms my soul, and I can appreciate the beauty of a simplicity that is priceless.

Ben is standing by the open doors that lead to a balcony with the most impressive view I have ever seen. Behind him I see a large table with cushioned seats pulled up to it and the table is set for breakfast.

Ben nods respectfully. "Charles and your lovely wife, Evelyn, isn't it?"

He smiles as he heads towards us and kisses me on both cheeks, and I almost swoon at how amazing he smells. Emma is the luckiest girl alive right now because this man oozes sophistication and allure and makes Charles look ordinary in comparison.

He regards Charles with a cool expression and I can tell there's no love lost there as he says tightly, "Come, we should eat."

Following him out on to the balcony, I stare around in awe as I take in all the trappings of wealth and success. It's obvious no expense has been spared in styling this penthouse suite and I'm in no doubt he will attract the richest of customers because this place drips luxury from its freshly painted walls.

We take our seats and Ben smiles. "Please, help yourself to tea or coffee, there's fresh juice if you prefer. On the side is the breakfast buffet and if you would like something hot, there's a phone with a direct link to the kitchen where you can place your order."

I am absolutely blown away as I head across to the table and select some fruit and natural yoghurt with half an ear on the conversation.

Charles sounds angry as he says tersely, "You've been avoiding me."

Ben's voice is emotionless as he says evenly, "I can assure you I've had more pressing items on my agenda. This could have waited."

"No, it couldn't." I feel a little embarrassed by the anger in his voice and look down as I concentrate on eating instead.

Charles hisses, "What was that text all about, you had better be kidding me?"

"It's no joke, Charles. When do I ever joke about business?"

"Then it's true, we've lost everything."

I look up in shock and Ben catches my eye and I recoil at the pity in his eyes before he faces Charles with a hard expression.

"Correction, Charles, *you* have lost everything, I have lost nothing."

"What do you mean? We were both in this together; you more than me and if I remember rightly, it was all your idea."

"It was but you see, Charles, unlike you, I keep track of my investments and as soon as I noticed a shift in the market, I instructed my broker to sell all my shares."

I can't even pretend to know what they are talking about

and I jump as Charles's fist slams down hard on the table, "You fucking bastard, it was you."

Ben leans back and regards him with a steely glint in his eye. "If you mean it was me who flooded the market with shares that were falling fast, then yes, guilty as charged. If you are referring to the fact that the stock lost its value inside an hour because of rumours of a fall in demand due to a lost government contract, then yes, you are correct. You had the same information as me, you just didn't act on it, how is that my fault?"

"Because I was on your fucking boat and there was no signal, you idiot. How could I act on something I didn't know because you put me there? When I finally got the signal and the endless texts from my broker, it was too late."

Ben nods. "Yes, that was most unfortunate."

"Unfortunate, I'd say it was fucking catastrophic."

Ben looks at me and says apologetically, "I'm sorry, Evelyn, this must have come as quite a shock to you."

Before I can answer, Charles slams his fist down on the table and roars, "A shock. That woman wouldn't understand what was happening if I spelled it out for her."

He turns to me and says bitterly, "What's happening is, we have lost everything. The savings, the house, the pension, it's all gone because of a sure-fire investment this man told me would make us rich beyond our wildest dreams."

Ben shakes his head. "Oh dear, it appears that you sank everything you own into it, that's bad practice, Charles, never put all your eggs in one basket, this shows you why."

"But…" Charles can't even get the words out as Ben laughs. "You say I told you to. Maybe I did, but you didn't have to do as I said. Yes, I implied it was a guaranteed investment, I may have told you that you couldn't lose and perhaps I exaggerated it a little but you see, I learned from the master."

"What are you talking about?"

Charles seems genuinely confused, but as I look across the table at Ben, I suddenly see why he's so successful. The friendly, easy-going manner has been replaced with a man with a heightened killer instinct. He looks as if he's about to pounce and devour his prey, and I am fascinated when I should be terrified.

His eyes narrow and his lip curls as he snarls, "You see, Charles, I have known for some time about your double dealings. The fact you have advised me on deals and done this exact thing behind my back. You have stolen from me, used me and thought me a fool."

The air is so tense I almost stop breathing as Charles freezes and words appear to have failed him.

Ben hisses, "You thought you had covered your tracks. You thought I had no idea of the shady business practices you use. The leaked information, the word in the wrong ear to suit your interests. The fact you manipulated the markets for personal gain and didn't care whose lives were affected as a result. If I feel anything, it's genuine disgust for a man who achieved his wealth at the expense of others. Well, you messed with the wrong man when you took my money and used it against me. But like every greedy bastard villain out there, you didn't recognise that the player was being played when I dangled extreme wealth in front of your eyes. You didn't see past that and protect the assets. You went all in and put everything into a deal you thought would set you up for life. You mortgaged your home, sold all your shares and cashed in your investments. You were going big on this because you saw a way of making more money than most people only dream about. In doing so you brought your house of cards crashing down, not me - you. Well, how does it feel knowing you've been played? Not good, I imagine."

Charles is apparently speechless and I look at Ben in

confusion and note his gaze softens as he looks almost apologetic. "I'm sorry, Evelyn."

Before I can even reply, Charles makes a strangled sound that appears to come from deep inside him and clutches his chest. I stare at him in shock as he turns red, then a weird shade of grey and grasps his chest.

"Charles." I jump up in alarm as Ben lifts his phone and barks, "Call an ambulance and send a doctor up here."

Charles makes a gurgling sound as he struggles to breathe and as he slumps face down on the table, I scream out, "Charles, oh my god…"

Ben reacts quickly and jumps up and, in a blur, I watch him pull Charles to the floor and start CPR. He shouts, "Evelyn, there's a defibrillator in the apartment, on the wall just as you came in, quickly!"

I stare at my husband lying on the floor, still and unmoving, and everything appears to happen in slow motion as I walk from the room and head towards the lift where we came in. My movements aren't hurried and they lack urgency as I walk towards the equipment that may just save my husband's life. As I reach it, the lift door flies open and a man appears and pushes past me towards the open window. I hear urgent voices outside, but I carry on as if in a trance as I gently lift the machine from its bracket on the wall. As my fingers close around it, I hear an urgent, "Evelyn, we need the defib, quickly!"

My legs appear to be stuck in quicksand, as I say loudly, "Coming."

As I walk back rather than run, I have only one thought on my mind, *I hope the miserable bastard's dead.*

CHAPTER 46

CHLOE

The resort feels different today. I'm not surprised because last night was intense, destructive and so informative. When John found me, we went back to the room, and I helped clean him up. He told me the staff had stood by and watched as the three men tore strips off one another. It was only when things started escalating that the security guards stepped in and separated them.

As I washed the blood from his hands and body, we talked long into the night about the past, what happened that night, how I feel now and life at home. I don't think we've ever spoken as much and when we woke, it was entwined in each other's arms with the slate wiped firmly clean.

Now, as we head down to breakfast, I'm surprised to find we are the only ones and as we sit overlooking the ocean, I look around me in surprise. "It's quiet here, do you think we're late, or early, I can't tell?"

John shrugs. "Probably early, I'm guessing the other couples are nursing big hangovers, or their pride right now."

Thinking about the revelations last night makes me wonder about the other people here. I wasn't the only one facing a bitter past, and I wonder if they have dealt with it as well as I have.

John says angrily, "Mind you, if Jack shows his face, I may be tempted to throw another punch at it. What that man did was…"

Reaching out. I touch his arm. "Enough, John, we won't speak about him, he doesn't get that right. I'm pretty sure he will have some explaining to do of his own, judging by that video we all watched. Poor Kim."

"Not really." I look up in surprise and blush when I see the woman herself standing beside me. From the look on her face, she doesn't have a care in the world as she smiles and the concern in her eyes makes me blink back the tears.

"Kim, I…"

John jumps up and pulls a chair across. "Take a seat, can I get you a coffee, tea maybe?"

"Oh, I don't want to…"

"Its fine, please."

I feel so bad for her because it must have been an especially hard night for her after finding out her husband was a sex pest, both in the past and present.

"I'm sorry, Chloe, what Jack did was unforgivable, are you ok?"

She looks so concerned I want to reassure her and smile. "I'm fine. To be honest, it was cleansing in a strange way. I never knew the identity of my attacker and now I can put a face to a monster and that somehow empowers me. It brushes away the darkness and leaves me with all the facts and gives me closure in a weird way."

"What about you, Kim?" John sounds concerned, which makes me love him even more.

"I'll be fine. Seeing it all unfold last night was devastating, and extremely hard to deal with, but it made my mind up - I'm never going back to him. We're now officially done and like you, Chloe, I feel as if I've shifted a huge weight from my shoulders and if anything, I feel free. Hopefully, that feeling will last and not remain here when I go home because I know I have a lot of changes to make in a very short space of time."

"What will you do?"

I feel worried about her, but she just shrugs. "I'm not sure. Probably move out, consult a solicitor, start divorce proceedings and move on. It all sounds so simple when I'm here and maybe I'm deluding myself, but I have to make some decisions and stick to them."

"Have you seen him?" I can't even say his name, and she shakes her head sadly. "I saw him last night and told him I was leaving him. It wasn't pleasant, but it had to be done. I couldn't carry on after what I saw." She sighs heavily and takes a sip of her coffee before staring out to sea. "I know he's left though."

John catches my eye and I say in surprise, "When?"

"This morning, apparently. When I left last night, I arranged another room with the receptionist. I had a note through my door this morning, telling me I could return to my room because my husband had checked out."

"How do you feel about that?" I feel shocked imagining what she must be going through, stranded in a foreign country on her own, dealing with a break up.

"I was glad, really. It's the best solution because it allows me a few days to think things through."

"Aren't you afraid of what you'll find when you get home?"

I can't even begin to imagine what that will be like, but she smiles sadly. "Not really. I'll go and stay with my sister while I sort things out. I'm done giving him more chances. They become meaningless after the fifth or sixth time."

"You're very brave."

"Not really, I'm just doing what I should have done years ago."

The sound of sirens interrupts the conversation and we turn and see a commotion in the reception.

"It looks as if someone's ill." John cranes his neck to look and I say quickly, "Can you see who it is?"

"No, just the paramedics, it looks as if they're being shown into the lift."

"That's terrible, I hope it's not one of the other guests, or the owner, it must be one of them, surely."

I feel on edge as we wait for news of even more drama and Kim says with a worried voice, "I hope it's not Evelyn, she was destroyed last night, the poor woman."

"After what she did to you, with your husband."

John sounds angry and I don't blame him, but Kim just smiles sadly. "I can't hate her for what happened. She's a victim just as much as you were Chloe. I spent a long time with her last night after it all happened, and I felt sorry for her above everything else."

We carry on eating and after about twenty minutes, the lift arrives and we watch as the paramedics leave, carrying a stretcher with somebody on it. I can't see who it is as they whisk them away into the waiting ambulance and John whistles. "That didn't look good."

"Why, what did you see?"

John looks worried and shakes his head. "Whoever was on that stretcher is a goner because the sheet was over his, or her face."

Kim cries out, "Oh my god, please don't let it be Evelyn."

As we fall silent, I feel my heart thumping madly inside me. This story isn't over yet. It certainly feels that way and I wonder what fate has in store because I won't feel safe until we land back home because this is turning out to be the strangest holiday of my life.

CHAPTER 47

EVELYN

$\mathscr{H}$e's gone. I watched the paramedics replace Ben and his resort doctor, and we stood by and watched the professionals battling to save my husband's life.

I think he was probably gone before they arrived. The look in their eyes told me everything I needed to know, and I suppose I was in shock because I don't remember sitting down and drinking the brandy that was placed in my hand. Ben sat beside me on one side and the doctor on the other as they absorbed the information the paramedics relayed.

I heard nothing.

I don't think I even registered the moment they left, taking Charles with them. My last memory of him is not a pleasant one, and I still can't believe that he's gone.

Ben is kind, just the way he holds my hand and looks at me with concern. The doctor equally so and asks me if I need anything for the shock. I'm numb, shell-shocked, and trying to understand what it all means – for me.

We have nothing – I have nothing. I understood that part at least. From the sounds of it, the house will be repossessed, leaving me homeless, and yet that doesn't frighten me as much as I thought it would. I was going to take that path anyway and so after a while I say quietly, "Thank you, you've been very kind. Would it be ok if I went to my room? I'm so sorry for the trouble, I just need to think about this."

Ben nods. "Take all the time you need. You know, Evelyn…"

I look into his concerned eyes and he says sadly, "I am so sorry you got caught up in this. I can't pretend everything will be ok because we both know that your husband gambled away everything you had. What I can promise is that I will deal with it all on your behalf. Don't worry about a thing, just worry about grieving and leave the rest to me. I'll make sure you're ok."

"Thank you." I don't know what else to say because I do need him. I need someone to help me through the endless red tape this is sure to wrap me in, and from the look of him, Ben is capable of making a hard situation easier. I know he feels guilty; that it's his fault, but I don't blame him. How can I, he was a victim just as much as me? No, I blame nobody but the man who has left a crazy mess behind him and I'm shocked to feel nothing but relief that he's out of my life for good.

Ben assured me I can stay as long as I need to, and as soon as I'm ready to leave, he will arrange the details. That's good to know because I can hide out here until the shock has passed. What it means for my future is no different than what I had planned, anyway.

It felt strange packing up Charles's clothes and possessions. A little surreal really, and I kept nothing at all. I handed them to the porter, who collected them because I asked Ben to just get rid of the lot. There's no reason for them now.

I spent the next few days in my room, seeing only the waiter who brought my meals. It was a special time because I can't remember the last time it was just me. Charles has been in my life for many years now and far from missing that, I'm loving every second. Does that make me a monster? I expect it does, but it takes a monster to shape one, at least that's what I like to believe.

Three days later and there's a tentative knock on the door. I know it's not the waiter because he left not long ago. I open the door and see Kim standing there, looking so worried I smile reassuringly. "Have you heard?"

"I'm so sorry, Evelyn."

Opening the door wider, I beckon her inside.

"Yes, it was quite a shock. It seems to be the week for those."

We head out to the balcony and I pour her a glass of the fruit cocktail I have grown accustomed to, and she looks at me with compassion. "Ben told us what happened, I hope you don't mind. I think he's worried about you."

"He's been so kind."

"Yes, to all of us."

I feel a little curious and she must sense that because she says sadly, "A lot can happen in a week. Life can alter on the tick of a clock and I doubt any of us will be the same again."

"What happened after?"

She looks out over the ocean like we did that fateful night and sighs. "Jack left, the next morning actually. I was sleeping in another room and never saw him go. It was fine though, I ended things the night before and now I just need to go home and clear up after the storm."

"And Chloe, what happened to her?"

"She's still here. She's happy though. John has told her they will be married as soon as he can arrange it, and I think that was all she wanted, really. It's funny how things work out. She had the family, but not the husband. We had the husband and one of us wanted the family and one of us

237

didn't want either. Then there's Ben, who wanted closure, to put his past behind him and move on. It was all pre-arranged. A crossroads to carry on a journey by leaving the baggage behind."

"What about Ben?"

"He's been so good about everything, which is ironic when he was the one who brought it all to a head. This whole week has been some kind of revenge trip for him. Closure for a past that affected him deeper than he realised."

"Emma's a lucky girl to have found a man like that."

"She didn't." Kim looks a little edgy as she shakes her head.

"Ben told me what happened with Emma. She was another part of his past that he needed to move on from. She hurt him deeply and she never even knew it. His plan was to see if she felt differently when she saw what he had become. If she'd changed and became less grasping and conniving. It appears she was still the same and was seduced more with what he could give her, than what she could give him. She left on the same plane as Jack."

"How do you know all this?"

I'm not sure if it's my imagination or not, but she blushes a little.

"Because he has kept me company most evenings. Maybe he feels guilty I'm on my own, but he's sat with me at dinner and we have talked over drinks at the bar. Not just me though." She's a little hasty to add, "Chloe and John too. We wanted to ask you to join us, but he told us you asked for space. I'm sorry, Evelyn, I couldn't bear to think of you here all alone and so I told him I was coming to see you regardless of your wishes. You don't mind, do you?"

"No." I smile. "I don't. It's good to see you and maybe you have room at your table for me tonight."

"Of course, we need to stick together, we all do because we share a bond now, the night our lives changed forever."

She looks concerned. "What about you, Ben told me Charles lost everything, will you be ok?"

"I thought the same. From the sounds of it, he risked everything we owned and some things we didn't. He left a string of debts and there was nothing remaining apart from one thing he obviously forgot about."

"What was that?"

"His life insurance. Coupled with the travel insurance he also took out; I'll have enough to buy a small house and start again. It's nowhere near as grand as what I had, but it will be everything to me. I'll find a job, anything to pay the bills and who knows, maybe I'll even be ok."

Kim nods and I know she understands. After all, we are both in exactly the same position and I know I've found a good friend in her.

Kim stays for the rest of the afternoon. We talk, laugh and cry and do it surrounded by luxury in the most beautiful paradise. Kim's right, our lives did change forever that night, for the better as it turns out. Life has a habit of doing that, the rough before the smooth, the good with the bad. It's how you deal with things that count and I learned a valuable lesson here and it changed me forever.

EPILOGUE

FIVE YEARS LATER

Ben

Where has that time gone? As I lean on the balcony and look out across the resort, I do so with a sense of pride. My dream became my reality and all because I never gave up. To be successful, you need to be ruthless, to be happy you need to be humble and kind. Material wealth doesn't matter if you have nothing behind it. The love of a good woman, a family to bring you joy and a thirst for living life to the full, whether it be surrounded by riches, or struggling to afford those little luxuries that make everything worthwhile.

The sound of children's laughter brings a smile to my face. Despite my initial plans, I grudgingly allowed children into the resort. It's still a luxury spa, but there are activities to keep the children amused while the parents indulge in luxury.

"Penny for them."

A familiar hand slips around my waist and I dip my head and inhale the sweet scent of the woman I have loved for five years already. She sighs and turns to face the view and whispers, "It all looks amazing."

"It does."

"So, this is the calm before the storm. Are you sure you're ready for this?"

Pulling her around to face me, I wrap my arms around her and hold her close, dropping a kiss onto her half-open lips. I will never grow tired of kissing this woman. Never stop loving her and showing her how much she means to me. Love has replaced revenge and laughter replaced the tears. My life is complete because I was so lucky to fall in love with the most amazing woman in the world.

"I love you."

She smiles up at me and I press her hand to my lips and smile. "I love you more."

We share a secret smile and as she leans against me, I relish every second she is in my arms.

"Daddy, daddy, I want to go swimming."

Laughing, we break apart and I lean down and scoop my daughter into my arms, tossing her high in the air until she squeals with laughter. My wife looks at us through misty eyes and I love seeing her rounded belly, swollen with a brother for Esme.

She laughs as she catches my eye. "She's all yours, I need to rest before Chloe and John get here."

"What about Evelyn and Greg?"

"They arrive tomorrow."

My daughter wriggles in my arms and I laugh. "Come on little one, let's leave your mother in peace."

As I walk away, I hear a voice say, "Don't be long."

Esme pouts, "Mummy, you can come too if you like."

"It's fine darling, mummy needs to take care of Louis, he's a little restless today."

"Will you be ok; we can stay if you like?" I feel a little concerned, but she just shakes her head and smiles.

"It's fine, go and have fun, I know where you are and anyway, we still have two months to go; if I can survive that long."

She rolls her eyes and I love the happiness that shines from them. Yes, Kim was born to be a mother. She was born to be my wife, and I was born to take care of my family and god help anyone who gets in the way of that.

The End

BEFORE YOU GO

Thank you for reading The Resort.
If you have enjoyed the story, I would be so grateful if you could
post a review on Amazon. It really helps other readers when
deciding what to read and means everything to the Author who
wrote it.

Connect with me on Facebook

Check out my website

Thank you

I feel very fortunate that my stories continue to delight my readers. The Girl on Gander Green Lane reached the number 1 spot in Australia in the entire Kindle Store. The Husband Thief and The Woman who Destroyed Christmas reached the top 100 in Canada, the UK and Australia.

I couldn't do it without your support and I thank every one of you who has supported me.

For those of you who don't know, I also write under another name. S J Crabb.

You will find my books at sjcrabb.com where they all live side by side.

As an Independent Author I take huge pride in my business and if anything, it shows what one individual can achieve if they work hard enough.

I will continue to write stories that I hope you will enjoy, so make sure to follow me on Amazon, or sign up to my Newsletter, or like my Facebook page, so you are informed of any new releases.

With lots of love and thanks.

Sharon xx (M J Hardy)

Ps: M J Hardy is a mash up of my grandmother's names. Mary Jane Crockett & Vera Hardy. I miss you both so much & wish you knew this chapter in my life.

The Girl on Gander Green Lane

The Husband Thief

Living the Dream

The Woman who Destroyed Christmas

The Grey Woman

Behind the Pretty Pink Door

The Resort

Join my Newsletter

Follow me on Facebook

Made in the USA
Las Vegas, NV
30 June 2021

25713998R00144